GRECH

GRECH

KEN EDWARDS

grand IOTA

Published by
grand**IOTA**

2 Shoreline, St Margaret's Rd, St Leonards TN37 6FB
&
37 Downsway, North Woodingdean, Brighton BN2 6BD

www.grandiota.co.uk

First edition 2025

Typesetting & book design by Reality Street
Cover and title page images & author photo by Elaine Edwards

A catalogue record for this book is available from the British Library

ISBN: 978-1-874400-94-3

ACKNOWLEDGEMENTS
Three sequences extracted from here ("Something happened",
"The Thought-glove" and "Luminosity") were included in
Bulverhythe Variations (photo book and recording, 2022) with
Elaine Edwards. The sequence "The Sluice" was published in
Golden Handcuffs Review 33 (2023) ed. Lou Rowan.

1 something happened

Something happened. There, where it happened before. What was it, when, where? *In media res*. In the wind. There as it blows. The wind makes our head cold and confuses us. There is almost constant wind here, where we sit or stand or lie, and it is chiefly blowing from the direction of the south-west, that is the prevailing direction, though sometimes (as a change) easterly, and one has to endure it, or make provision against it, or go with it, as is appropriate at any particular instant; for sometimes it's mild, it softens the cheeks, glorious to relate, and sometimes it's horrid, but that's how it goes. It goes and it happens. That is, it sings. It sings as it sounds. A high-pitched sound in our ears, or that may merely be the tinnitus. And we sit or stand or lie in our quarters, which are partially sheltered, it has to be said, which will do. We are *in media res*, which is Latin for in the middle of it all, or in the middle of nowhere. We are discovered here, or we are in a position to be discovered, but to be quite frank we hope not to be, we sincerely hope to continue our life with as little fuss as possible. We lived in a house once. But our quarters here, they will do. For the time being, which is all the time we have in any case. Our quarters consist of a shelter, provided unwittingly by the Council, that is to say, unwittingly in the sense that it was not, one has to admit, originally intended for this purpose; the Council in no way intended this shelter to serve as our quarters, and so one has to admit it has been repurposed, without the Council's knowledge, let alone express permission, but has been standing for quite a while, it would seem, though the paint on it, which is green – to be more precise, Buckingham Green – is fairly new; and incorporated into the shelter, which is of sturdy construction, is a bench, originally intended for the benefit of the public (who no longer frequent this location much), on which we sit for most of the time (when we are not walking about, or when we are not ensconced within our tent), where we might be discovered but would sincerely prefer not to be. For we forgot to mention we have a tent (contents of tent to be enumerated at a later time). And the tent is of a blue colour, sufficient for a single person, with a zip fastener on the entrance, meaning the slit by which we enter its enveloping sufficiency. And the tent, pitched by the side of the shelter, on the leeward side, that is to say the side protected from the prevailing wind, that is on the right-hand side of the shelter as one would observe if one had one's back to the sea, is of sufficient quality for its purpose. We have not yet mentioned the sea, which is of course a continuing presence. Nor the beach, for that matter. Which is always visible, and palpable. It is made of stones. It is a long shingle beach, not much frequented these days by holidaymakers, who prefer sand. But to return to our quarters: a tent is all one needs. Or something like that. Except in conditions of extreme weather, perhaps in the depths of winter, when other temporary arrangements would have to be made. Although this winter that we have recently endured, that we are coming out of, was relatively mild, so that was of course fortunate. We lived in a house once. But it didn't work out. Hey ho. Whatever. Built of brick, falls down. That's the law. The bricks fall down. Eventually. However they do. Howsoever. But it wasn't the wind that did it. It wasn't the wind that blew the house down, that caused *that* sound, the catastrophic sound that echoed all along the foreshore, that caused the gulls to go up in the air. That was definitely not the wind, that terrific destructive force that brought the house down. We are not referring specifically to the house or houses wherein once we dwelt, which to all intents and purposes may survive, almost certainly survive today, wherever they are, though now inhabited by others. Almost certainly. Though nothing survives forever, is what we were working up to saying, but what a banal point. What a banal point to make. It's the kind of thing Grech might have said. No, we will not use the G— word. We try not to think about G— these days, but it is not easy. Nevertheless. Where were we? The first house was a house of straw, remember that? I will blow your house down, the wind says, I will huff. I will puff. I will weather you down. And the next house was a house of wood. And the wind says the same. And the house after that, a house of brick. Same result, the wind says and sings, as it does. Never you mind, I will do it. I will do it, if it takes years, I will, sings the wind, prevailing from the south west, as it does in these parts. Never mind. It has to happen some time. Every time it happens. The bricks make a certain sound when they fall down. Now all of this is by way of leading up to attempting to describe the event that disrupted the peace that afternoon by the beach, the event that opened this discourse. The sound would have reached our ears almost immediately, it was that close. It was a sound clearly audible above the high-pitched sound of the wind, above the sound of the sea. It was a catastrophic sound, one that had not been heard before, more clearly audible than the rush of one of the trains as it approaches, as it swoops past, on the line behind, on the beyond section of the chain-link fencing complex, so no, it was not a train, definitely not. We have not yet mentioned the chain-link fencing, nor the trains. One hardly notices them after a while being stationed here. But this, certainly not a train by the sound of it, aside from which we are familiar with the timetable by now, we have internalised it, so can exclude that possibility, this was entirely new. The bricks make a sound, above that of the weather, the moving weather. The moving weather within the climate, which is a structure built of weather systems, how they circle. Make circles, that is, of sound and motion and much else. That sounds good, make a note of it. Though it may not be of use. May not be to the point. We are straying from the point. Which is: the falling bricks make a sudden sound, startling, out of kilter with the ambient sound and the recurrent sounds. That's what happened. And then later it happened again. After it had happened before, well then, blow us down, it happened again. And it set all the herring gulls into a flap, the bricks falling down like that. But they did not fall; they were pushed. There were men working, that was the reason, they had been there for a few days, they'd been noticed, up towards the east of this vantage point, set up with their vehicles next to the beach around the construction site, which first had to be a destruction site, because there can't be one without the other (construction and destruction, that is, another example of co-dependent binaries, about which we'll have more to say later), the site anyway boundaried with security fencing and warning notices for many days before *that* sound came, proclaiming that the building was suddenly in the throes of being brought down, with great smoke billowing. The assembly of yellow machines in the day leading up to it should have served as a warning. It went unheeded. But the herring gulls certainly did not like that. It was a shock. They made their displeasure plain. That's how that happened. It happened, and happened again. There was shouting too, there were warnings or cries of alarm. What cries? Who was crying out? The men or the birds? They flew up in the air. The birds, of course. Chaotic, turbulent moments. And then the men and their machines had another go. And the gulls, leaving their own stations on the various roofs around upward of the beach area, shouting with great emotion, fly up in a great pandemonium (or palace-of-all-the-demons), a hullabaloo, what to do what to do? they shout. They are silvery-grey and white, with their pink legs and yellow bills, and they fly around the grey and silvery early spring sky in one turbulent moment after another. And now the wrecking ball came round once more, smacked that old building in the face again, whack, and down come more bricks, bang bang, and up go the gulls. Well, the gulls are shocked, truly they are, by this repeated transgression, this invasion of their quotidian abyss, and they're all talking about it, as we know, for we know them well, the several pairs that had been beginning over the past week or two to snoop around the rooftop sites of their old nests, feeling that time come around again, the time for refurbishment, to get it on and give evolutionary processes another prod, that is to say, in short, they'd been thinking of baby-making. What were they saying? The wind is one thing. That is what it will do. It will sing, for all it's worth. But this, this was an outrage. A human intervention, an egregious display, a violent demonstration of the law of entropy, that is to say the transition from house (on whose roof there might have been an opportunity for nesting, for baby-making) to mere bricks. And all the king's horses and all the king's men are powerless, not that the herring gulls give a great deal of anything for king's horses or king's men, no more than we do. From house to bricks, that serves as a classic demonstration of the second law of thermodynamics, as the birds in their abyss understand very well, and as will become better understood, except that understanding itself violates entropy, so it's always a long losing battle. But a calm is coming. It must come, surely. The gulls resettle. The men took no notice, of course, engrossed as they were in their tasks. We know each one of them – the gulls that is, not the men, whose meanings and motivations were obscure to us at this point; they are starting to settle – the gulls – they are resuming their pair bonds right now, where they were *wont to build their bower*, as they have been these past few weeks, the pair on the garage roof to the left, the pair on the building overlooking the derelict and abandoned beach huts a little further on, the others from yet further afield. The building that was being dismantled had not, so far as can be determined, itself functioned as a breeding station. So it wasn't a question of anybody losing their homes, in this instance. It was a building whose function was never clear. Reality is not what it seems. What is it, what's it doing, the gulls' hullabaloo? It's just a response, that's all, a response to threat. The fading light drinks it all up. *In media res,* in the middle of the whole bloody thing, or in the middle of nowhere. So after that there was quiet for a while, the smoke settling on the piles of collapsed bricks, just the occasional shout from the men, but this interleaved with moments of renewed calm. And what it was, the men were packing up now, for it must have been approaching four o'clock in the afternoon, and at this time in the early spring the light would be beginning to fade across the beach; we were still some way off the solstice. Their machines had been turned off, the juddering had stopped – the juddering having come into consciousness for the first time precisely because of its sudden absence, precisely because previously it had been an unremarked feature of the aural environment, an underground rumble not otherwise perceived. That's how it happens. The yellow machines, tarnished by rust. The machines would be good for another day, but the bricks, of course, were now in a more than somewhat disordered state; the collapse was considerable. (We have read recently by the way that there

is a 90% chance of human society collapsing within decades, but we are not in a position to make a meaningful
assessment of this prediction.)

Peace returned to the foreshore. Our flock seemed finally
pacified, anyway. The men were all gone now, having
knocked off for the evening. Something happened, that was
all the gulls knew. They would have already forgotten about
it, in fact. Our friends the herring gulls, of the species *Larus
argentatus*. They are, as even the naturalist Tinbergen, who
loved them, acknowledges, not that bright. But in our own
mind the memory trundled and acquired freight along the
way, in a manner not altogether welcome, but for a while
below the level of consciousness itself. Something occurred,
and then faded into the past. And so evening drew on – a
snack that had been snuggled away previously was consumed, the last of the contents of the Paisley-patterned
thermos flask was drained, the bladder was relieved behind
the rocks way over yonder, the teeth were scrubbed and any
residue spat onto the shingle, the tent was readied, blanket
gathered together about oneself. And all these preparations
were being made for the night ahead, as usual, when the
next thing occurred. It was an internal occurrence this time.
Something else – call it a thought – occurred. It slapped us
on the face, metaphorically. Pah! Call it a thought. An idea
or opinion produced by thinking, or occurring suddenly in
the mind. Well, that's a rather circular definition. (Idea?
opinion?) But here it was, anyway. The nub of it was this. If
there had been destruction, this thing called thought went,
it must surely be followed by construction. For what would

have been the point of going to all that trouble? The assembled machines, the cohort of personnel, the time taken? To simply remove a redundant building? For no reason? It had been there, mouldering, evidently for many years. No, there would be more to it than that. Construction must be being planned. For certain, almost for certain. But how to obtain even more certainty? More detail? There might be a notice, possibly a copy of a planning application. Or a public information notice. A notice that would provide the relevant information, unwelcome though it might be with its implications for our future status. In short, what was the plan? These things have to be faced, unfortunately. Such was the inner discourse. Thoughts like these never wander aimlessly into their own private domain to be lost forever; no, these were rigorous thoughts, of the type that assemble themselves into sequences that make sense; sense of a significant nature, with potential consequences, impacting right here. And now. There was a need for more research, anyway: that had been established. Yes, there were almost certainly notices on that site, it may now be recalled, that had previously been overlooked, that might repay further study in order to discover any clues therein as to the purpose behind this demolition, and what phase two, shall we say, might be, once phase one, demolition, had been achieved. But now dusk was gathering, and such a foray to research the facts further would not just be another irruption of an unwanted nature into normal procedures and protocols for the evening, but would also represent a considerable effort in terms of discerning any available small print; and it wasn't of pressing need anyway to do this, to walk the fifty or a hundred metres to the now deserted site, to try to make out what was going on (if any of it was legible, even printed or written down at all), and to walk all the way back. It could easily – more easily – be done in the morning, and there would be no significant disadvantage. This is how the thoughts were going, along these lines. Thoughts tend, one finds, to gather momentum as dusk gathers, as the number of passers-by, never great around here, around this rather desolate part of the beach, diminishes even further, and we are left alone with them, the said thoughts, here in the abandoned commonwealth of consciousness. Yes, these are fair thoughts indeed; they would undoubtedly pass the Turing test with flying colours, dare we say, they would without question establish our humanity. At the very least. There is life here yet. Circumstances may be diminished in scope compared with previous times of plenty. But there is every reason to believe that, seasoned with an admixture of seasalt, our thoughts as we dwell here are becoming stronger, more spaced out in time, clearer, less hurried or jumbled. There is more chance than ever, one feels, of arriving at sound and reasoned conclusions, of reaching mature judgements, untainted by partiality, bias, attachment, bad politics, affairs of the heart, prejudice, racial or other hatreds, congealment of attitudes, naivety, blindness to the facts or excessive reliance on irrelevant variables. To achieve such a state would be to live well. To be content to hear the wind bluster and make no comment. No question of that.

But having noted all this, the wind and the waves seemed to have died down towards evening, from a roar in their daytime pomp to a hush, with the occasional isolated gust providing a late flourish. That was the way it was going, on the evening that is being spoken of. The evening following the double crash of bricks. A sort of *diminuendo*. *Poco a poco*. Throughout all of this, the tent had stayed firm, pitched as it was in the lee of the shelter, as has already been described. The only interruptions: the trains, on the other side of the path and the chainlink and barbed-wire fence. At this time of the evening there would be just two an hour, one in either direction, the up and the down. The rush of that, but you don't notice it after a while; it's just like the waves, a *crescendo*, the climax, then a *diminuendo* back into the distance of memory, reduced to the dimensions of a punctuation mark. And that double rush per hour is in a different time signature from that of the waves, which we haven't mentioned before. Well, they may have been mentioned in passing, or they may have been implied. The sea we have certainly mentioned. The sea is always there. It doesn't need to be mentioned. It's always happening. There – where it happened before. Even in episodes of high wind, the waves never quite reach us. The beach is wide and commodious enough to prevent that occurring, even at high tide. The sea is not the ocean – that lies to the west – but the English Channel. Admittedly, a storm surge, in excess of eighty or a hundred miles per hour perhaps, if it were to coincide with an unusually high tide, might pose an existential threat to our station. But most of the time we are all right, it is safe enough. So it was that evening, an evening like any other, except inasmuch as nothing is like anything else. At these times the sea is more *frequent*, obviously, by which we mean the waves are, because the waves are inseparable from the sea. It depends on whether you want to think in frequency or wavelength. So the evening wore on. A little more chill. It was at this point that the decision was taken to get up from the bench in the shelter, have a last look, a last shuffle around and then retire to the tent. The torch was checked: still some battery life left. There was always more reading to be done. A last look along the shoreline, then, past the garage to the left, the beach huts a little further on, the building site just past that where there was now a pile of rubble, and to the right the continuation of the pathway that passes this shelter, no bicyclist or pedestrian there now, and beyond, the headland, and then at the back of us the railway line behind the fencing, with the pedestrian bridge over to the west, and the further buildings behind that, and at the front the beach and the sea, which shall eventually, we hope, be described in all its immensity; but that will have to wait for the mental and imaginative resources to permit. A gloom coming over all this. It was by now quite cold. This past winter had not been too bad, we have already mentioned, it was only now and again that refuge had had to be sought, when the *kene cold blowes through my beaten hyde*, and the *wriggly tails wagged*, and all of that, but it was at this point that we would look forward to the spring. It was at this point. That was the point of it. But what was that out on the horizon? It's always grand to behold the vessels that stand out, as they pass, always from left to right, from east to west, for that's the shipping lane visible from this vantage point. We love to watch them. If we had an emblem, it would be an anchor. There was a particularly large vessel now visible through the gloom, standing on the horizon – so we quickly grabbed the treasured binoculars from within the tent – a pinprick or two of light maybe visible on its superstructure but mainly consisting of a wall of cargo packed into standard containers of many shades stacked maybe as much as a dozen high and twenty across which if you were hard up against it would have the overwhelming effect of an immensely tall building. And all stacked tightly onto the hull, black and low-seeming with the block capitals M S C painted thereon, but actually itself the height of a considerable building. So, a ship out at sea, a container vessel, noted. And another beginning to appear to the left of it, following it, probably a tanker, and at the extreme left yet another like it, but not so large. Almost a fleet, in fact. All heading as always towards the mighty ocean off to our right, westward ho, heading into the prevailing wind, which was by now very much dying down, as has been explained. It seemed from time to time that a considerable metropolis could be discerned on that horizon. Houses might be imagined. Slowly moving cities might be imagined. But enough. They were, one by one, quickly disappearing, stage right or is it stage left? into the greyness that enveloped the distance at this time, and would soon be forgotten. The enduring appeal of "a boat across the water". Soon gone. Too many ideas. They thrust themselves into the brain, and need to be resisted; it is not good for the general health. No, it was time to turn in, zip up the entrance to the tent, get in the sleeping bag, turn on the torch for some reading before the visit of Sister Sleep. She would be arriving from a long way away, as always. The visit of Sister Sleep, sometimes though rarely accompanied by Sister Dream, was always to be welcomed. Deep alpha waves alternating with rapid eye movements, in that familiar rhythm, that was the hope for the next seven or eight hours. One would then become, as we all were once, no more than a column of air like any other. But a ship out at sea, a fleet, a house, a creak. All these useless elements. And the sea itself? As we have noted, it is always there, that is the principal feature of it, just the being there, and so there it was again that evening before retirement, the sea, which has not yet been adequately described (for it's beyond our powers at present, or at least our inclinations), just being, and the evening now flows into night. Best get in the tent, was the thought. The evening had come. It was passing away. As it always does. The houses that nestle well away from the shoreline started to close in. We felt we were falling. We found ourself falling. It was a familiar feeling; it has been extensively described elsewhere so there is no need to elaborate. But suffice it to say, immersed in the ocean of consciousness, we have felt this way for some time now. When you have descended for some time, the floor eventually, inevitably comes to greet you. But this, like all other phenomena, will pass.

2 a general inventory

Those of us – not many – who dwell on, near or around the blessed segment that forms this part of the foreshore, or who habitually frequent it, will start to be in evidence from the first light of day. There are the twin fishermen off to the west – emphatically not part of the mainstream fishing community further away, the quaint one that the tourists come down from London to photograph – these two brothers often begin to mend their punt and their nets before dawn, making their way silently to and from the island of low broken buildings out of which they work. They form a maverick and impermeable family of their own; nobody we know has ever engaged in informal discourse with them for many years. They don't say much, either to each other or to the world at large: just a low grunt maybe, now and again. Very occasionally what may be construed as a groan. By this time some of the herring gulls have begun to give voice too, perhaps articulating frustrations of various kinds. It is their manor, after all. And we too will have emerged into consciousness, or at least into a different mode of consciousness. We may by now have emerged from the zipped-open flap of the tent, feeling the cold sting of the air on our bleary eyes, on the skin of our face. The sky still indigo, not doing much. The waves just whispering, so the gales of the day before have not returned. Something happened. *There* was where it happened. What was it? Best not think about it first thing in the morning. It's customary to walk up and down for a bit, before getting round to sitting on the bench. What some have termed distracted lurking. Listen to and feel the sinews and the bones creaking. Tinkle upon the stones. Blessed relief. The east was reddish, there was more creaking, but that new creaking was not from the sinews or the bones but emitted by an early cyclist approaching on the path that tracks the chain-link fencing and passes behind our station, his front light in the still gloom bobbing now with the unevenness of the surface, the periodic breath becoming more audible with the approach; they are various, the cyclists, and this one, a male of advancing years, did not acknowledge us but swept by without commentary and vanished in the direction of the buildings, creaking still the while. The same direction in which the building site, or more properly *un*building site, was to be found, of course: that was the something that happened, of course, and consequently was the unfinished business for the morning. It was good to have that identified and marked. It would be attended to in due course. But before that, the next occurrence scheduled was the first train of the day, initially heard rumbling in the distance, then quickly approaching from the east, rushing past and vanishing with a Dopplered roar into the west, which is the up direction, and which instantly fixed the time at 06:13, with an estimated five to ten minutes then to wait for the sunrise, already gladdening the eastern horizon (so that was a promising sign for the day), and in attendance for which a sit-down on the bench was customary. Indeed the breeze was only slight, and brought with it faint odours of fish and sewage. They always seemed to emanate from the rocks around, and also the remains of man-made structures that now stood out in intricate detail in the dawn light, but equally were unfathomable in kind, compositions of knurled aggregate and strong cement with a shapely snag or two, and those flint walls on the far side of the railway topped by broken glass. And the final episode of what might be termed the first phase of the morning, as the colours were already beginning to infuse all the surrounding features of our environment, was the arrival of the runner. Typically preceded by a steady footfall on the path, in a rhythm both sturdy and dependable, the runner on appearance was as always slight and female in shape, wearing on this particular occasion a luminescent pink singlet and black jogging pants, her dark, faintly silvered hair held in a band, white earbuds in place, a pair of dark glasses on her face, faintly glistening; and it was customary for her to give a slight nod of the head as she passed, to which an acknowledging nod from the bench was the appropriate response. And this indeed is what happened on this occasion as on so many others. For she might be said to be kindred. A rare, kindred spirit, but one with whom we only ever had glancing contact and never exchanged a word. And with that was concluded the initial proceedings for the early part of the morning. They occurred in what was now officially day, and in the light of day. That was to say it all came to light, just as it came. There as it ought to be. It was a democratic light, available to all at no charge.

Approaching now, a familiar voice registered: You all right, my love? Wind's stopped anyway! Sharonne – the spelling is not certain. It may be Charonne, which would suggest the feminine equivalent of the character that punts dead folk over the river of the underworld. Unfairly, because she might best be viewed as a ministering angel, of which there was probably a lack in the classical nether regions. Her familiar ruddy complexion and solid build notwithstanding.

You're looking pretty good this morning, she went on, did you have a nice night? It was tolerable, she was told. Sister Sleep, we informed her, had paid a mostly uninterrupted visit of at least seven hours, which is the very best we can hope for even in times of calm, let alone during such stormy weather. Sharonne bore in her hands the replacement thermos flask. This morning it was the burgundy one. They alternate on a daily basis, it must be explained. The Paisley-patterned one, now drained of all its contents, was handed over to her, and the exchange took place. Sharonne has been tending to our needs for many months now, the flask being spontaneously produced at an early stage in our relationship. For a long time, its contents had invariably been sweet tea, until at long last the subject had been broached: coffee would be most welcome, coffee with milk but without sugar, if that were possible. Course you can, she had cried, with all the goodness of her heart. And so after that it was coffee – indifferent, it has to be said, insufficiently strong if the truth be known, but recognisably coffee. So this morning as all other mornings the hot, fresh coffee in its burgundy container was handed over. And thanks were given, as always. For that, and other kindnesses. The donation of a cagoule. The odd bit of advice, whether taken or not. The bringing of news from elsewhere. There was then a lull in the conversation, while the first sips from the mug that doubled as a flask-top were enjoyed, while the early spring weather was mutually enjoyed. Side by side we sat on the bench. Then, indicating the sea she had been staring towards, Sharonne commented: Like satin, it is, ennit? And to think what it was doing yesterday. Which seemed as fair a simile as any. Better as a description than "wine-dark" anyway. Like satin this morning. And so the sea was mutually contemplated in silence for a few moments. The first couple of gulps having hit the spot, the thermos was again sheathed, if that is the right expression, the throat cleared. The shenanigans of yesterday afternoon were then mentioned. The sudden noises that had startled the flock, emanating from the building site towards the east, towards which we gestured. Did she have any further information about what was going on?

They been pulling the houses down int they, dear? What they're gonna put in their place, Lord knows.

This was of course the concern at the heart of it. We discussed our proposal that, as part of our daily foray for the purpose of ablutions this morning, we intended to detour in order to inspect the site for any indication of plans for it, plans that might impact on – well – that might impact. That might have an impact. She understood what was being said. I heard it was gonna be holiday homes, she ventured, but I dunno. That would put an end to your peace and quiet, wouldn't it? We agreed that such a scheme would indeed have that effect. Your peace and quiet is quite important to you, ennit, she stated; quite so, we agreed. But what can you do? she went on. We said that we did not know. She was solemn; then her demeanour brightened, for *clowdie welkin cleareth*, as the poet said. She stood up. OK darling, she said briskly, I'll be seeing you tomorrow!

Morning ablutions. Once again, we need to think about this. Or do we? It has become habitual, one supposes. So overriding any decision-making. The brain finds ways to minimise activity. So much the better for that, but what if the situation changes? As it did previously. There used to be public facilities near the beach here, which we made use of, three toilets in a row, though only the disabled one worked, which was an irony. But they were closed down and locked up by the Council a while ago, and that happened suddenly. There had to be some urgent decision-making then. And there is a need to be permanently vigilant: who knows how long the present arrangements themselves will continue to be available? The decision-making in respect of such necessary activities, well, that is obviously complicated, the more so, one realises, when one reads about the brain processes entailed: the orbital cortex becomes involved when the question is what to do; the lateral cortex becomes active when the question is how something is to be done, and the dorsal portions of the particular lobe mediate when to do it. And so on. Extremely complex when you think about it, but clearly the preference is not to think, because that uses up energy and interferes. On the other hand, it is important not to let custom and habit take over, precisely because of the likelihood that the present circumstances may not, will not last. The possibility of taking a different route to the place of ablutions each day, just to keep the neuron connections supple and ready for change, has occurred to us, but the route choices are extremely limited. Hence the routine. To sum up. A solution was found after the previous crisis, after the Council closed the public facilities, citing a lack of public funding. The upshot is that morning ablutions now normally take place at St Anthony's. It is a parish church, twenty minutes' walk from our station, which is not ideal, but it serves. The powers that be there are sympathetic to the needs of those with no other resource. A sacred place, St Anthony's, but then all the bodily functions are sacred, if one wants to imagine it in those terms. Holy holy holy, the tongue and cock and asshole holy, and so on and so forth, as a poet once proclaimed. Defecation, micturition, washing of the face and hands, scrubbing of the remaining teeth, all of these activities take place currently on hallowed ground. (Shaving has been allowed to go into abeyance for now.) There are even fresh towels, there is soap provided. But to get there, that requires decisions, or required decisions initially, though they are now normally taken without much pause for thought, which as we have suggested is dangerously complacent. First, it must be remembered the quarters have to be abandoned – that is the major consideration – the blankets and the cushions left on the bench to advertise our claim, the blue tent zipped up. At this hour, which is still early for the majority of the population round here, it's low-risk. But still, there is some danger. The valuables, such as they may be, are taken with us. But there are not many, of course. It isn't clear what constitutes a valuable. In practice, not too many items are taken. Then there is the route to be traversed – but again, there are not many realistic variables to be had in this respect, as we have shown, so decision-making is relatively easy, and in practice, as indicated previously, increasingly reserved for the subconscious processes. The direction is principally eastward, into the sun, if sun there be (which this morning, the morning we are describing, was the case, so care needed to be taken not to be blinded; a pair of sunglasses might have come in handy, but we currently possess no such object, so keeping the head down had to suffice). We had considered maybe varying the route from day to day, as a means to keeping the neural pathways active, but without many viable options that course has tacitly been abandoned. The landmarks along the route, then, are, first, the edifice known to all as "the garage" which has been shuttered in all the time of our residence, and in which it's unknown what kind of vehicles are kept; next, the beach huts, in fact a beach hut shanty town, a double row of identical structures with canted roofs, distinguishable by the alternating pastel shades of their frontages, now closed for the season and it appears for all time, judging from the state of them, a rutted road providing access on the leeward side for the one-time holiday-makers who no longer come; beyond that, the wasteland where the remains of the building that had been there until yesterday now lie this morning, reduced to a huge pile of bricks, the whole of it presently encircled by temporary fencing and cluttered with machinery. We passed in front of this on our journey to St Anthony's this morning, observing that a small van had just pulled up in the road alongside and two men had got out, the advance guard, ready for the day's work. They seemed exceptionally vigilant, shouting instructions to each other with sharp voices. We had been hoping to approach the site and investigate whether any planning notice had been affixed to the fencing that might shed some light on the prospects for our future in this neighbourhood. But the men didn't look as though they would be especially friendly, so after some thought the site was skirted carefully, and once again earmarked for later investigation. And then beyond that, the main road, freighted with (not too heavy at this hour) traffic, curving towards the beach; and so round the corner, hidden by the frontages of a terrace of gaunt houses, we came to the public park in its hollow, part sheltered, because set at a lower level, from the prevailing winds coming out of the sea. You have to descend to it from the beach promenade by means of a small ramp. This was where we had once set up camp, before retreating to a safer, because more out of the way, location further west. For right in front of the bowling green was another Council-built shelter, the analogue of the one beside which the tent is currently pitched, its bench and stanchions the exact same shade of Buckingham Green, if perhaps a little fresher, a little less weather-beaten, a shelter within which we were previously domiciled, until the level of traffic of people going to and fro, approaching and receding, became excessive, and we were obliged to retreat to somewhere less in the way. This shelter had subsequently been claimed by another denizen of the foreshore, but only briefly; it's not clear what happened to him, whether he had been moved on by the powers that be, or had left of his own accord, or had become a casualty. At any rate, this morning it was clear of belongings, and available for any member of the public who wished to sit there, though at this hour nobody had taken up this opportunity. The bowling green behind it, abandoned, presented a scruffy appearance following the depredations of winter: the grass inconsistently lush, badly needing mowing, as did the pock-marked lawns that were interrupted hereabouts by shrubbery, by stunted dragon trees (of the genus *Dracaena*) and by a winding path. It was hard to recall that six months previously, at the high end of summer, these lawns and this bowling green had been parched and showing different shades of brown. There were few people about. But we could not tarry; our need was becoming greater. And so we approached St Anthony's, a brick-built arabesque edifice in bad need of repair, suffering from years of exposure to the prevailing, salt-bearing winds from the sea. When you reach it, you go down some steps; there are seven in each short flight. The objective is the crypt, as it is called; it smells musty, of course. There are alcoves here which may once have held tombs, or alternatively aquaria peopled by exotic marine life in ancient times. Who knows? Somewhere, accessed by a side door, there is a small auditorium, with a stage, unused most of the time. Once, we did hear muffled sounds of music coming from there. This would have been one of those rare occasions where our visit took place in the evening. We could discern the thud of a bass, the sounds of saxophones, a drumkit, a piano. On investigation, we found a jazz workshop taking place. A heterogeneous group of older and younger men, and one or two women, were working their way through the Great American Songbook, with variable results. We stayed to listen, standing silently in a corner. One of our favourite tunes was played, "On Green Dolphin Street"; at least we think it was that, though the uncertain intonation from some of the novice horn players threw some doubt on it. "Autumn Leaves" was definitely played, and a bossa nova that was instantly recognisable but to which the brain could not put a title. The workshop leader, a grizzled man with glasses that glittered, whose instrument was alto sax, prone to uttering gnomic comments between the tunes, presided benignly over the session. The rhythm section consisted of a battered drumkit and a battered standup bass played by solemn-faced older cats with the demeanour of Easter Island sculptures. A lady played the piano, which was slightly out of tune (not her fault). Three fellows in addition to the leader: trumpet, alto sax and tenor sax, and a spirited lady playing soprano sax. They played for about an hour and then a break was announced. We were welcomed at the interval and offered tea in a china cup by the grizzled leader. Biscuits were passed around. We were asked if we had come with a view to joining the session, which took place, we were informed, every Wednesday evening, and had to reply that, sadly, we possessed neither an instrument nor the requisite talent for playing one. We were told we were welcome just to listen. However, the call of nature took us away in the second half. That group has not been encountered since, but then our visits to St Anthony's only take place early in the morning these days. Once or twice we did make the trip specially on a Wednesday evening, but the room was dark and empty, and we wonder if we misheard, perhaps it was a Tuesday or a Thursday that the sessions took place. Sometimes still as we pass that door on a morning on the way to our ablutions we hear the muted reverberations of their sounds, the crash of the cymbal, the slightly out of tune chords from that upright piano, the harmonic meetings of alto and tenor saxes and trumpet, the thud of the bass – we tune into and out of these ethereal sounds which appear to emanate from a long way away but are in reality manifesting now only in our memory. So to return to the present, we did not take that side turning into the music room, but proceeded to the usual facilities. These are primitive but serviceable. Here, hot water gushes from the taps into great cracked ceramic bowls, but they have to be primed for some moments first. Showers are available – they take minutes to arrive at a tolerable temperature. The toilets have chains dangling from the high-level, rust-spotted cisterns, which need a good tug. That you are rarely bothered by well-meaning folk is a blessing. Once we were introduced to the Rector, whose name is Jeremy, and who seemed quite inoffensive as well as alarmingly young. He was the one said to have been on TV once. That his face was instantly familiar, of this we are almost certain. It was an eager, open face in which the lineaments of well-meaningness were everywhere evident, a face that tried so hard. General questions were asked about ourself, about our background, which we evaded successfully. He insisted that we and our kind (by implication) were always welcome to the facilities of St Anthony's. Lunchtimes they were open. We tried this once or twice. If you're lucky you get a sandwich sometimes. A better prospect is the hot meal at the Shell Beach Project, but that is a further walk still. Anyway – to return to the present once again – there was nobody about, the ablutions were all performed once again, all as normal. Emerging afresh then from the abyss into the March sunlight – it's almost certainly March – one was assailed anew, the last vestiges of Sister Sleep removed from the eyelids – the sunlight edged with purple – by dialogue and congress. Booming bass frequencies, for example, emanating from a travelling car sound system, Doppler-shifted as the vehicle moved away, proclaimed the virtues of lusty love. The body purged, the things that fester forgotten again, our legs drove us once more to the little park before the sea, where it was thought to be a good idea to sit on that bench for a while – not the bench that was our home, but our previous domicile in front of the bowling green – to relax the sinews, the bones and the sinews and the muscles, for a short while only, to balance the honey and the gall, while groups representing the local human race started to gather and mingle in that morning that was just getting going. A short sojourn, then, with the intention afterwards of reverting to the home station, where more peace, more space was to be had. And so the park came once again into view. An intermezzo, one might say. Was that the buzz of a bumble bee? No. It was in fact the sound of a light aircraft that grew in the sky until it was overhead and visible, or would potentially be so were one to crane one's neck and peer into the brightness. Barely visible. If only the binoculars were with us, if we had only slipped them in the capacious pockets of the coat. The bench in the park was still vacant, anyway. Good. But the binoculars would only have drawn unwelcome attention. They were best left where they were, in the tent at best guess, unless they had been stolen. Which is always a possibility, but we have to mitigate risk. So, to sit down on a bench that is not one's own. (Not that the usual one is either.) It makes a change. An occasional chance to observe a wider range of humanity, with minimised risk. We had the notebook with us. A few people walking their dogs; they're OK, they will pose no threat. For example, a stocky young man, the sides of his head shaved, in a dark hoodie and shorts – the weather, clement though it is this morning, scarcely calls for this sort of attire – guiding, or being guided by twin black pugs individually straining on their leads on the path. At the far end of the park it says DANGER NO ENTRY in red block capitals on a white ground, the structure beyond the railings being out of bounds. Everybody avoided this area. A bench such as this is always a good vantage point from which to observe how human subjects perform slow dances, selecting trajectories that never intersect catastrophically but weave between, without collision, without there apparently being any intention involved. It is a marvel, when you think about it. Among the others this morning, there was also a familiar grey-haired woman, in a grey coat today, with a plastic carrier bag, her little dog of the terrier type on a lead, the other hand bearing an electric-blue plastic extendable scoop with which she was picking up rubbish here and there and deftly depositing each selected item in the bag, for what purpose it was not obvious. This time she came up and asked our name. She was given this information, but the opportunity to ask her intention was missed. Pleasantries were exchanged, anyway. It is well to oil the wheels of human interaction. Further afield, two very young children moved erratically on the path on their little pink and blue bicycles fitted with guide wheels, under the distant supervision of a mother figure who was engrossed in a mobile phone conversation the whole while. And a sullen teenage girl with bearded beanie-wearing dad. We are making assumptions here. Two youths or maybe a little older, shall we say young men, sauntered in our direction, one with short dark hair, pale complexion and a neatly trimmed beard, the other of a more dusky hue, a little taller, lanky you'd say, both in deep conversation. Most people would like to go, probably, said the first. Take a break, they'd tell me, probably. You'd see that this is very contemporary, replied the other. How we live. And have to continually feed, you know what I mean. Most people believe that.

The sulky teenager was meanwhile shouting to her father: That's what *you* ought to weigh! He replied: Body-mass index, that's very misleading.

The dark lanky young man, almost simultaneously: Long ago, the hunters, and the gatherers. They believed that, in them days. But that was in them days. Yeah, most people would say that, said the bearded young man in response. But what would you do?

Go probably, take or leave it, you can take it or you can leave it, you can come and go.

But go?

Yeah, go, I think.

Teenager and father had meanwhile resumed their walk, at a metre or so distance from each other, receding into the background. The cry of the teenager could still be heard from afar, still addressing her father: It's bigger'n I fought it was! she cried suddenly.

But what I mean, said the lanky one, realism is way weirder.

You're not kidding, replied the other.

Now a variegated group of youngsters could be seen coming down off the promenade, quite noisy, a babble of accents. At the tail end of their conversation one said: What was that all about? And this, as so often, was followed by much forced laughter. It was all quite harmless. It's later in the day that the risk factors begin to multiply, but we shall not go into that. The plan was to retreat to our station, after this little interlude of research into human interaction, to spend a pleasant afternoon reading on the bench (that bench, "our" bench, not this one), in the pleasant sunshine that is promised. It was something to look forward to, and there is little enough of that to be had. After a short spell taking notes, it was felt a good time to retreat; the atmo-

sphere was starting to become mixed; as more people started to circulate the particles were beginning to move in
strange currents. This is how the thoughts were going. You
have to assume that everyone's infected. On the way out, it
should be mentioned that chalked shakily in blue on the
pavement below the ramp was the hopeful and forlorn message NO RACISM. An injunction, or a statement of fact?
Not the latter, assuredly. But meanwhile, one last observation, a small group of ringed plovers, *Charadrius hiaticula*
if we remember correctly – grey-brown backs, white aprons
and the black and white rings round the neck – might be
observed scurrying around, oblivious to the human world
gathering around them, occasionally burying their little
beaks with savage stabbing movements into the grass verge
beside the promenade.

We are home again at our station. Our quarters. All is well.
All checks out. On the way back it didn't prove possible, as
had been anticipated, to get close enough to the small print in
the notice that could now be observed, very likely a planning
notice, stapled to an upright inside the building site fencing.
Once, we would have had the capability to investigate, we
would have had no fear. But now? The eye of the supervisor
was fixed in our direction. This is private property, the eye
was saying. Clear off, it was saying, that baleful eye, without
actually saying it. It seemed prudent to withdraw anyway.
Perhaps after four, when the men had knocked off for the day
again? Perhaps the light would still be good enough? We still
had the torch, anyway. They were now involved completely in
reducing the huge pile of bricks and clearing the rubble from

the day before, shovelling, directing a digger that was spooning it all into the back of a truck. One was loudly whistling "When a Child is Born". In March? Oddly unseasonable. Yes, directly after four, the light would be starting to fade again. But if the torch were to be brought and focused on the notice? Though the eyesight is not good these days, even with such aids. Hard to accept the loss of our powers, that is to say our powers of agency, of direction. We have declined, there is no doubt about that. We were an agency once. We were an agency, and we investigated. We even led an investigation team. We solved crimes. It's hard to believe. And we had a library once, of some thousands of volumes, a library that could be located, visited, browsed, looked after, re-ordered by topic, genre, author's name or any other system one might devise, perused, catalogued, added to, trimmed, rebuilt over and over. Now down to three or four. The remnants. Three or four books left, maybe five at most, out of all those thousands, but that is an unconfirmed estimate. Just three or four or five books, insofar as they can be counted, can be catalogued, it's not absolutely certain what the number is. We have them here, somewhere. A search can be instigated, anyway. But while we're at it, well, it may be helpful to make a general inventory. Helpful to whom? For what? For what purpose? An inventory of what? A search of what? That's easy: of possessions to hand – accepting that there may exist also other possessions currently in other persons' hands, lawfully acquired or otherwise. (We know this to be the case.) Setting aside what we mean by "person", which we shall return to. And we may return, too, to the specific person in mind, whose name shall not be repeated here, though it may have been let slip accidentally. So, to commence. Let the record show that on such and such a date in the month of March, which we strongly believe it to be, there were to be found the following. One single-person tent with integral groundsheet, blue in colour, capable of being rolled into its own bag together with its aluminium framework: the donation of benefactors (The Shell Beach Project). Two blankets, of different sizes, one of a plain beige colour, the other bearing a motif of a bird, which is the favourite. Two cushions, shabby, dull pink, which may serve as support while seated at the bench or as pillows at night within the tent. One sleeping-bag, dark green. One towel, pale blue and white stripes. Two spare pairs of underpants and five assorted socks in addition to those being worn, two of them especially thick, two with holes in the toe. Two T-shirts, dark blue and off-white, in addition to the shirt being worn. A heavy sweatshirt, of an indeterminate dark colour, currently being worn. A pair of cargo pants, dark grey, currently being worn. Shoes (well-used Nike trainers), currently being worn. A substantial coat, a little threadbare but hanging together, of army green colour, currently being worn. A cagoule rolled up in its black waterproof covering, the gift of Sharonne. A baseball cap, faded blue, currently being worn. Alternative headgear for the cold, in the shape of one woollen beanie, currently crushed in the pocket. Eyeglasses, with soft case. One toothbrush, yellow, in a small bag together with a half-full tube of Colgate toothpaste. One plastic beaker, one plastic plate, both dark blue, and a selection of white plastic cutlery in a clear plastic bag. Two small sachets of Kleenex tissues. One burgundy-coloured, slightly chipped thermos flask, by the feel of it still half-full of no doubt by now lukewarm coffee; this item not technically part of the inventory, in that it is on loan from Sharonne for twenty-four hours. If this inventory had been compiled twenty-four hours earlier, or twenty-four hours hence, the item would be Paisley-patterned. One plastic torch, used chiefly for reading in the sleeping bag at night, and a selection of spare AA batteries. A pair of small, cheap Minolta binoculars, without the case, a more expensive pair having been lost or stolen. And here is the mobile phone, of the dumb variety, which we had once presumed lost, but was there after all, though not presently operating. At the Shell Beach Project we were asked whether we possessed a mobile phone. Do you not have a mobile, mate? – you are correct, we reply, that we do not have a mobile if one were to assume the question referred to a mobile phone that worked, because indeed a moment's ferreting would probably disinter a mobile phone that is non-functioning; that is what our response would have been. And so here it is. And part of the reason it's non-functioning is that of course there is nowhere in these quarters to plug it in, to extract the electricity that would charge it, with the assistance of the appropriate plug and lead; but the chief reason it's non-functioning is because this procedure would be redundant in any case because its inner workings have possibly been fried, possibly irretrievably, and this happened quite some time ago. But that may not be so, it may be that it's a simple question of purchasing a new SIM card. It's fair to say that. So the answer to "do you not have a mobile" is both quite simple and quite complex. To continue, anyway. A shabby black wallet containing a five-pound and a ten-pound note and sundry change – there may be more change in the trouser pockets. A bulky and battered manila envelope containing documents and photographs. A cheap wristwatch, non-functioning (it really should be thrown away, but for our concern about waste). An assortment of ballpoint pens and pencils, the latter with the tips broken and therefore, because lacking a sharpener, currently of no use. A collection of six notebooks, ranging in size between A4 at the upper end (ring-bound, pale blue lines, scarcely used apart from a few pages covered by diagrams the meaning of which presently escapes us) and smaller than A6 at the lower – two of them of the sort manufactured in the People's Republic of China in the 1980s, black with a red spine, one almost completely full of dense hand-writing comprising a journal, the other half-completed – and the remaining notebooks filled to a greater or lesser extent, or conversely, empty to a greater or lesser extent (a philosophical point we shall not belabour here). All of these presently employed for the purpose of entering these logs and composing these lyrics of the strand. To carry the bulk of these possessions, excluding the tent: a rucksack, black, weathered, capacious, and a holdall of rough beige canvas, with both a handle and a carrying strap. And so we come to the library. It appears after extensive investigation that there are in fact only three books remaining. First to hand, *Towards a Science of Consciousness*, a hardback volume of some seven or eight hundred pages in extent, dustwrapper intact, fifty-five contributions covering the topics Philosophy of Mind, Cognitive Science, Medicine, Experimental Neuroscience, Neural Networks, Subneural Biology, Quantum Theory, Nonlocal Space and Time, Hierarchical Organisation, Phenomenology. Second, *The Herring Gull's World*, by N Tinbergen, paperback, cover chipped and somewhat faded towards the spine, 1971 reprint on 100% recycled paper. And lastly, a nineteenth century edition of Spenser's *Shepheards Calender* (Containing Twelve Eclogues Proportionable to the Twelve Months), spine ends scuffed and split, tanning along spine and board edges, light scuffs at corners, tanning and foxing to endpapers and text block edge, well presented, very readable. No other books can be located at the present time. We had been optimistic that there might be a few more left, but it is not so. The others must therefore be presumed lost. In conclusion, we do not own a telly. Nor, any longer, a computing device of any type.

3 the thought-glove

Sister Dream pays an unwelcome visit, and we are lost again. When we are in the tent, perhaps with light rain drumming relentlessly on its roof above us, "pent up here in the dark" as another poet somewhere says, we lose perspective. We have no working timepiece, so we can only estimate duration – it was probably an hour or two before dawn when we woke from the dream. The worst time. The circumstances of the dream have quickly dimmed, though the dream-affect remains strong. Our circumstances in reality, or what passes for reality, take time to re-register. Our hold on existence, that is, especially here in the dark. But if we try hard we can retrieve some detail of the dream from afar: as though we are peering through our binoculars into the figurations of distant fantasy, where nothing quite makes sense any longer. There is at the heart of this dream a dreaded individual, an ever so familiar being we cannot bring ourself to name, a monster, a nemesis, perhaps one of our own creation, fashioned from the clay of our imagination. This being, though coming from far away, appears now to be in the tent with us. *It* lives in the tent. *It* was once far away in spacetime, and now suddenly resides close by once again. *It* is a complex being, as well as monstrous, lies on the bed, turns its head to us, though this creature *is* also us. There are separately articulated parts to *it*, that is to say, *it* can be divided into features, appendages, attributes. There is a logic to its construction, however strange. But there it is. *Ipso facto*. The monstrous object in the dream, that's what we are trying to recall. It has a name, a very familiar name that we have heard on numerous occasions, but can't bring ourself to utter right now. G-g– no, we can't. A being we reject. But now, as wakefulness returns, thankfully, it has gone away. Just so far away, but no further. None of this exists, does it? Has never existed, will never exist. What exists is this immediate reality. Only this. Only the sea, imagined outside the tent (it can be heard), and a few small shellfish and stones, and the gulls, briefly dormant now, just a small grumbling sound from them now and then, and the patter of water droplets on the canvas above. *Ipso facto*, and *sui generis* to boot. Maybe water is all there is. The sea runs far away, and then the tide turns, and it's suddenly much closer. As close as it is. As what is? As what *it* is. We're going round in cycles. We have not yet described it. Because it can't be described. It's far away and yet right up in your face, and still you can't see it. You will know it when you see it. You will know it when you hear it, or smell it. It's just what you can say it is. Some may say it's a clue, the background to all this, to the narrative, if that's what this is, but it isn't. It's not in the background. There's no background. There is only foreground – what else can there be? What else can exist? We are all water. *That* is water (the sea, the rain), but so are we. We must believe there is an order in things. One follows from the other, creating an emergent property, so the scientists say. That is one theory, consciousness is an emergent property of the brain. In the interstices and fundamental workings of the brain, a cosmos is always emerging. We are dimly aware of that world, a cavernous world, the one to which Sister Dream holds the key, and which she shows us nightly, with perhaps some respite from time to time, but it's one that fades as soon as the door to it is closed and the key turns in the lock. We crave as well as fear that world, but all of it has been lost. Again. All that happens now is these sentences. Sentences filling the void. Sentences come out of our body, continually. They make their way into the notebook and stare back at us. We've had enough. We just never want to read that sentence again. Not even *that* one, the one we cherished? Come on! The second half of it at least is very beautiful. But that is irrelevant. Ebbs and flows. *That* is water, *this* is too. We are all water, that's it. Go with the flow, as they say. And with the ebb. Socks off, socks on. So far, so good. Better: so far, so far. What sentence was that?

The Angel, we try to avoid. The clientele there is not conducive. To what? to civilised discourse, on the whole. Although there are pockets of it occurring from time to time, when you least expect it, let's be fair. And one cannot eschew completely human discourse, even of the most debased kind, it's what makes the world go round, where would we be without it? But more pressingly, we tend to avoid the Angel because we have insufficient funds these days to purchase strong liquor, or liquor of any kind for that matter. The Angel is a public house, a matter of some ten minutes' walk inland from our station. It has been there for generations, centuries even, so they say, having changed its name on more than one occasion, though it's admitted by all that it has seen better days. There are rumoured to be mummified cats and rats entombed in its walls, as was the custom, not to mention the fossilised remains of first-generation video games, their spectral pings still hanging in the air forty years later if you listen closely. Watercolours of the sea by a local amateur hang crookedly on the walls. The toilets bear the scent of the marshes. The present landlord is unspeakable. There are living, enduring presences too, though; for instance that of Hairy Bob, who resides there most of the day, every day, watching the world go in and out of the pub, perched grumpily on a stool in his special corner at the end of the bar with his eternal cup of tea and a small glass of something strong to hand; for all that his appearance strikingly resembles that of the average denizen of the street or of the foreshore – a fellow we might otherwise have met in our own peregrinations, likewise lacking the liquidity for liquor – he is not what he seems. He is rumoured to be a rich man. We were speaking of civilised discourse and its lack; with Hairy Bob, it has to be said, civilised discourse (at least, that is the impression one gets) is something to be rationed parsimoniously, as are all other commodities in his world. That was the secret of his success, back in the day. Parsimony, that is. Possibly the secret of most rich folks' success. So some say. But where were we? What was the point that was being made? Once again, things seem to have drifted. Yes, the clientele of the Angel. Some of them have formed the impression our name is Phil; how this came about is not clear – it may have been a series of Chinese whispers – but inertia caused us to let that go, and so we are "Phil" to all intents and purposes in this particular social context. It was a long time since we previously attended, but here we were again, thinking we might have enough for a drink, thinking it might do us good to disburden ourself of current anxieties caused by all the crashing and banging on the foreshore and all that that implied for our future presence there. You all right, Phil? barked the ginger man whose name is Angus, spotting our entrance from the corner table where he was ensconced with his life companion and also a third party, who might be Mickey Two Suits. (He was at any rate wearing a particularly smart one, if a little faded, double-breasted in a blue pinstripe.) You all right? repeated Angus who has been barred from the pub on more than one occasion but had on this occasion successfully served his most recent period of probation, and is always friendly enough until the day when he isn't. A glass was held aloft. You could look through it. Come and join us, he invited. Half full or half empty? was our enquiry. I'm a half full guy meself, he asserted, addressing the world at large. It can only get better. Oh, was the reply from the third party (Mickey?), it can get worse, *much* worse. What do you say, better or worse? What do you say, Phil? One of the two. It's got to be one of the two. Sit down here, will you? So what brings you in here, Phil, we ain't seen much of you for a while.

Angus' on-and-off friend and companion Queenie, a little woman with a red face and iron-grey hair cropped short, joined the conversation: All right, Phil, she said eagerly, all right? you all right? We could only nod in response. You're the same and different. You're always the same but different. Whichever you pick it will be the worse for you.

Doesn't sound too good, then, was the general opinion.

We therefore launched into an abbreviated version of the story: the great crash, and then the second crash, and other noises after that, and the understandable reaction of the gulls, the partly thwarted investigation into possible causes, the building site, the rubble where once a building had stood, the notice of planning permission granted, the certainty, the inevitability of building works after even more demolitions, building works encroaching further and further onto our space, and finally the impending ruin of our sanctuary, our realm of thought and contemplation.

There was concern, sympathy all round. What you going to do? inquired Angus, and it was explained there was probably nothing to be done about it, there would have to be a measured retreat at some point in the very near future, but plans were yet to be formulated

D'you have any people what can help? Two Suits wanted to know, and the response was that bridges had been burned, that the past, which was a very different place, was of no use now, that there were now few people in a position to help, though soundings would have to be taken. And that led the group into considerations of our past, both immediate and remote, a route we had tried to avoid in previous conversations. Where d'you come from, then? said Queenie, who was evidently already in her cups – normally quite a shy woman, but the accumulation of beverages always unlocked her tongue and put fire in her belly – where d'you come from, Phil, I mean origi-nana-rally?

Originally?

She meant originally, clarified Angus.

Shaddup, you ginger drunk twat, *I'm* speaking to him.

Arcadia, we said.

Arcadia, where's that?

Somewhere in Greece.

Ah, Greece! How lovely! You Greek, then, Phil?

Mickey Two Suits said: That explains it.

Or nowhere.

Beg pardon?

Greece, or nowhere.

Ah. Was you ever married, Phil? Did you ever have a wife, or ... you ever have a girlfriend? cried Queenie, and our considered response was, yes, we had a lady friend once. Back in the day, as they say.

What was her name? she asked eagerly.

We said, after some thought: Tabula Rasa.

What's that again?

Tabula, her name was, we said, *Tabula Rasa*, by coincidence it's Latin for not much going on.

Did she speak Latin, then?

Not well.

And what about Greek? She didn't speak Greek?

Not one word.

And so what happened there? she inquired – why, what happened, nothing, we said, well nothing much happened, you're barking up the wrong tree there, or sniffing down the wrong hole, or whatever is the most appropriate metaphor. It was a long time ago, a very long time ago, and we no longer had good recall of that time, we explained, in the sense of which event preceded which, and which was the cause of which, and who was to blame, and so on and so forth. And it is fair to say Queenie's repeated questioning was beginning to stir up memories that were far from pleasant and that we would prefer to lie down again and go to sleep.

Tabula ...?

Rasa, we repeated.

Did you call her Tabby, is that what you called her? Sorry, I hope I'm not intruding on grief, or bereavement, oh no, Phil, I didn't mean to do that (placing a small hand on our arm, as if aghast at whatever transgression she suddenly realised she might have committed), oh I'm so sorry, Phil, please forgive me.

It's all right. Tabula Rasa went off with Grech many years ago.

Who's he then, Grech?

We had not meant to mention Grech. That was a *faux pas*. Unwise. The name that we try not to utter. Because likely to lead to misunderstandings, unwelcome inspection, the tedious need for explanations, qualifications, detours through the dream rabbit warrens of time. Why this? Why that? This explains that, and that explains the other, a never-ending chain we can't be bothered with. We had to come up with something. So we replied to her question:

A friend.

Not much of a friend if you ask me.

No.

D'you see them at all, your ex and this Grech geezer, d'you see them?

Not for a long time, we asserted, there are issues there, we explained.

Stop interrogating him, said Angus, intervening again.

I ain't interrogating, I'm having a con-ver-sation, right? That's what it's called, you wouldn't know nothing about that.

There was a touch on the shoulder.

Phil, Phil, why the long face? Can we cheer you up, Phil? You all right with that drink, Phil? You don't wannanother?

That was Cliff, who had just come in, a weasel-like man with tanned skin and white hair. Mr Clifford Edgeworth himself, former punk musician. Only, you've got a bit of a pallor on you today, are you feeling quite yourself? he asked with concern – a question to which there is no sensible answer.

He's got the hump, said Angus.

What about?

He's had bad news.

His gaff is under threat.

Is that so, Phil?

Planning permission for twenty-four holiday and family homes, comprising one- and two-bedroom flats and three-bedroom houses, we recited.

Twenty-four? Do you mean on that building site where they've just done some demolition? How can they get twenty-four on that site?

Well, apparently they're going to demolish them beach huts too, said Angus on our behalf.

You don't say! That's outrageous, they can't do that.

They can, we said, and they will.

Cliff said: That's really close to you, then, innit? Really close to home.

We reaffirmed this.

Maybe, said Cliff, this is your chance for rehousing. Have you thought about that? Shell Beach done me proud, got me own flat now, as you know. Very nice. You should take it up with the Shell Beach, you never know, Phil. They're very helpful. The Shell Beach Project, know what I mean?

Unlike the bloody Council, said Angus.

Hear hear, said Two Suits.

Yeah, the Council, affirmed Queenie, you'll get nothing from them.

The conversation meandered onto the question of the various conjunctions of circumstances in which "they", that is to say the authorities, often personified as the Council, always get their way, at the expense of "us", that is to say the common people, and how the cards are always stacked the same way. It began to acquire a familiar, disjointed air.

Speaking of which, chimed in Mickey Two Suits, you ever hear from Ali the Turk? Didn't he take the Council to court? That's what reminded me.

Ah, Ali, said Angus, I seen him last Wednesday in town, actually.

How is he?

Moderately OK, far as I could tell. I just saw him briefly.

Only, he could talk, old Ali, that's what I remember. The hind leg off a donkey. Big old Ali, the twenty-stone virgin, ha ha. Wasn't he writing a book about his life? Yeah, some of them old guys, you used to see them in here all the time. Now you never.

Yeah, him, and Six-Fingered Sally, but you never see her now either. Have you seen Six-Fingered Sally, somebody was asking last week, so I said, No, haven't seen her recently, but actually, funny, I was thinking about her just the other day.

Ooh, that takes me back, Six-Fingered Sally, whatever happened to her?

She was a complicated woman.

Women. They're all simple and soft or hard and complicated.

Angus! Never heard such a sweeping statement in all of my bleeding life.

Haven't you?

Fucking hell, I never.

Anyway, there warn't nothing complicated about her, old Sal.

Hundred years gone by, she kept saying, hundred years gone by, whatever did she mean by that?

This was no longer a conversation in which we could usefully take part. Besides which our present resources were exhausted. So we stood up, thanked the company for their concerns, bade our farewells, retrieved from a capacious coat pocket the baseball cap to shroud the luckless pate, and with that, preparations were complete for the premises to be abandoned. All of this while Hairy Bob was still perched in his corner of the bar, supping slowly and silently his tea (as always with the little tot of something stronger on the side), in his personal porcelain cup and saucer specially provided by the management, glaring peacefully at the world with his flint-like blue eyes, visible through luxuriant, snowy whiskers, that watched us as we crossed his view, as we left the pub. And we saw a glint of recognition there, just for an instant, as we passed. It was almost like looking in a mirror. A kindred spirit, or something more sinister? But that was just an illusion. Not a lot is known about Hairy Bob. They say he used to be a banker once. So they say.

Here where we now find ourselves, on the beach with no agenda, no way forward, we are subject to forces over which we have no control. Nameless forces constantly fly through the air and grow until they eventually destroy everything we once knew. They destroy, or, you could say, *destory* it. Just change the position of two little letters and there you have it. So there was a story there once, but it was cut. We had it all, the narrative once intact, all memory of it intact, insofar as memory ever can be, but the forces, which could be physical or economic or historical or medical, whatever, perform a *narrativectomy*. But that's the way it is. This is how progress happens, by deletion. Natural selection. Maybe embrace it. Why do we need all that ponderous backstory – away with it in all its broken mendacity, let us disburden, offload, take flight; for example let this that was immediately perceived as a threat, the demolition and the proposed encroachment on our territory, the *twenty-four holiday and family homes, comprising one- and two-bedroom flats and three-bedroom houses,* all of that nonsense, be viewed instead as an opportunity for liberation, an opportunity for us to depart and find new fields, unencumbered by all the apparatus of modern commerce, further from the centre, but where? where? we shall find it yet, but first we need to dispense even more radically with past narratives, and in so doing fully commit to *destorying*, to *narrativectomy*, hah, yes. These coinages appeal. Are they apt? We have no idea. Because we have no *ideas*. That's good. That's a start. Because without ideas you have to rely on thought. Thought may well be embedded in the universe – Einstein said this – but ideas are its bastard offspring. There are too many *ideas* cluttering up our brain. If you have an idea, if an idea occurs to you, well, you may think, what to do with this now? what on earth to do? you can't imagine what to do, so hey, let's have another idea. Put another idea next to it – bad move. They proliferate unhelpfully, these ideas, these *stories*, they get worse and worse, from one iteration to the next, yes, it could be said ideas have been the scourge of *civilisation*, the name we give to the lamentable state of affairs we see all around us and which shows no sign of abating. Good idea? Bad idea! So it goes, forever. They solidify in time, these ideas, good or bad originally, into ideologies or *isms* – we have no end of them. Why, we have monotheism, polytheism, antitheism, atheism, agnosticism, monism and dualism; and more specifically Taoism, Tantrism, Buddhism, Shintoism, Confucianism, Hinduism, Sikhism, Judaism, Zionism and anti-Zionism, Hassidism, Kabbalism, Muslimism and Islamism, Wahhabism, Shiism, Sufism, Zoroastrianism, Catholicism (of the Roman kind), Orthodoxism of various sorts, Protestantism in general, and specifically Calvinism, Lutherism, Methodism, Unitarianism, Quakerism, Baptism, Anabaptism, Mormonism, evangelism, and all the way to antidisestablishmentarianism; and not forgetting gnosticism, Manichaeism, occultism, creationism, theosophism, pantheism, animism, paganism, shamanism, secularism, Satanism. And we also have capitalism, imperialism, conservatism, monetarism, liberalism, anarchism, anarcho-syndicalism, socialism, Fabianism, communism in its various forms, specifically Marxism, Leninism, Stalinism, Trotskyism, Bolshevism, Maoism, and all the way over on the other side Naziism, fascism, and, facilitating all this, terrorism, tribalism, populism; but also Utopianism, feminism, humanism, pacifism, monarchism, loyalism, unionism, nudism or naturism. And furthermore, modernism, imagism, realism, surrealism, Dadaism, cubism, futurism, fauvism, Vorticism, suprematism, symbolism, romanticism, impressionism, expressionism, constructivism, objectivism, atonalism, serialism, minimalism; and how could we forget atomism, rationalism, materialism, monadism, empiricism, Cartesianism, positivism, reductionism, scientism, essential-ism, relativism, idealism, vitalism, determinism, cynicism, scepticism, nihilism, dogmatism, formalism, existentialism, solipsism, Epicureanism, Stoicism, and also Darwinism and neo-Darwinianism, Freudianism, behaviourism, Platonism and neo-Platonism, and also extremism of every possible variety – not to mention all the many *schisms* that occur within all of these. Once the *ism* has been attached to the original idea, it's already dead, and worse than dead, it's worshippable as well as buyable and sellable. Everything becomes shit, or, to quote our friend Mr Clifford Edgeworth (of whom more very shortly), becomes a load of wank. This is the trouble with ideas. They degenerate. Away with them all! Best to have no ideas, only pure thought, and then the thought can grow stronger, as we believe may be the case in these times, at this location, that is to say here on the beach, on the bench or in the tent, but it could be anywhere. It could be elsewhere. We could go elsewhere. The particles of our world are starting to reassemble in novel ways. Pure thought, uncontaminated by ideas with all their lurid connotations and consequences. Footprints on virgin sand. Not that this describes our beach, which is mostly composed of shingle, as may have been previously observed – it's a metaphor, obviously. Go back to the beginning, before all these ideas started coming in and messing things up. *Da Capo*, back to the beginning, start again. Which is not Latin but Italian for from the head, or out of one's head, or making it up as you go along; well, actually, a poet said that, and they have licence, don't they? They have poetic licence. Meaning, they have licence to make it up, though many of that poetry tribe also have too many ideas, and *that* spoils their poetry. Best break it up and make it appear as if out of nowhere. It's not literally true, *Da Capo* doesn't mean that, of course, but do we have to spell it out? Our own thoughts are growing and developing each day, though they are not poetry, we concede that. But the best poets have no ideas but speak through their words, through their arrangements of language, whose function is primarily aesthetic, no ideas but in thought, and its flow, which is eternal, which does not solidify. We no longer have examples readily to hand, alas, our library being so severely depleted. But we aspire to that, most definitely. They are not necessarily *saying* anything, these poets, any more than music is *saying* anything, but just is what it is. Music is our chief lack here, our chief regret. We long for the sound of a full horn section. Or even a trio of trombones. We reflect with nostalgia on that jazz workshop session at St Anthony's, previously described, even though the quality of playing there was not necessarily of the best. We don't count the garbled fragments of entertainment noise that leak from portable devices carried by visitors to the beach from time to time, particularly during the summer months. It's partly for that reason we stay away from the more popular sections of the beach. But music ... the gulls furnish something of the sort, in their own way, though they would deny any aesthetic function (if they were in a position to deny anything). They are in fact wonderfully melodious, without seeking to be, maybe because not seeking to be. They are out of time. Out of what we consider to be time. In free time. And they make it all out of the air, that is, the air around them and flowing into and out of their bodies. Music is the other side of the air, says Rilke. Somewhere, he says that. Somewhere. Maybe nowhere. We are unable to check. Rilke is a poet we are very much in sympathy with, but alas, we no longer have any examples of his work to hand, here on the beach, only what sticks in the memory now, and the memory is fallible. At one time our library possessed several different translations into English of his poetry, each with their own merits and defects, but those volumes have unaccountably disappeared. The library is no more, or almost no more. So it goes. In this oasis we have come to. So it goes and so we have come to, the same old thing. So the same, so they say. What are we talking about? Descending into gibberish once more, but no, keep your nerve, hold hard, once more unto the beach, dear friends, once more, or close the wall up, with what, the dead, as always, the dead are always with us, the English dead, here on the beach, or wherever we find ourselves or will find ourselves at the present time or at any future time. Well, all this talk of music and so forth reminds us that Cliff, that is to say Mr Clifford Edgeworth, lately encountered at the Angel, had on a recent occasion visited and sat on the bench with us, this very bench where we write, to pass the time of day and listen to the gulls. For he was appreciative of their music too. He had not made an appointment: his familiar dark narrow face and shock of white hair just suddenly appeared beside us, but the appearance was not unwelcome. A long face with the emblems of death written in it, yet very much alive still. And juglike ears, sticking out, very attentive. And so we listened to the gulls together. All the various sounds that comprise the full richness of their musical vocabulary. The familiar keening mew that they emit year round, their quarking if you like, which is picked up as if by contagion by others, their necks stretched forward as they utter it. Then the low choking and grumbling. And the alarm call. Also the squealing, whining, begging call, which the young will start to emit, but which the female also produces to beg food from her mate. The trumpet call, which one hears around this time of year, springtime, starting always with low sounds, then subdued high notes with the head pointed down, and finally, with the head thrown upward in a sudden jerk, the mouth wide open, a definitive series of loud, resounding screams, the body shaking; our observations confirming that this call is produced not just in the throat but by the entire body. All of these noted and appreciated. We would explain to Cliff that these cries are each activated by an internal urge, when the symmetry of the birds' being in the world is broken, when they might be imagined to experience what we humans call strong emotion, emanating from a significant lack of some kind; and Cliff would listen intently, a gleam in his eye, his stick-like body tense with attention. He was after all actually a musician, or had been, he told us. A punk, he said, proudly, of the original and purest and most radical generation. As we contemplated the tankers and freighters on the horizon, he related anecdotes, some of which he had related before, sometimes slightly differing on first or second repeat, of the time he had been in a band that had had some success, which had brought with it unwanted consequences he called *pressures*, that had eventually resulted in the disintegration of all that had been built up. Mr Clifford Edgeworth, well known back in the day as Unstable Cliff Edge because of what he called his death wish, which was evident in many of his lyrics, had forgotten much more than he managed to recall, and it was doubtful if all his anecdotes were one hundred percent accurate, or even fifty percent accurate, but they formed a viable if broken narrative. It might be said that he was the prisoner of his broken narratives, but who are we to judge? What had been the name of his band? The band was named Suckling Rats, if we recall it rightly. Almost certainly Suckling Rats, and he, Unstable Cliff Edge as he then was billed, played lead guitar and shared songwriting. These were vaguely familiar names, though this was not the sort of music that had ever been our principal focus – noise, disruption and insistent 4/4 beats at in excess of 200 per minute being its chief characteristics. He still received all these years later an annual payment into his bank account from the publishing company, he said, not a huge sum, but not inconsiderable, comprising royalties for that year, mainly emanating from the two semi-hit singles the band was remembered for.

At one time this would have been his only income, though now supplemented by the state pension. The bass player, long dead, he said ("drugs" he said), had been called Shammy Leather, but the *noms-de-guerre* of all the other band members, who came and went, are lost among the ruins of memory. Cliff said he had given away or sold all but one of his guitars, and no longer played even the remaining one very much, because of his arthritic fingers. He said he listened mostly to Scarlatti these days. We wish we were in a position still to listen to Scarlatti. He trembled when he got excited, a blurred replay of the wild-eyed shimmer of his vintage stage performances no doubt, and had mental health issues to this day, he reported, bipolar he said was the diagnosis, modified and more or less stabilised by medication now. He was at pains to tell us that the world at large usually only saw him when he was tending towards the manic; he completely withdrew from the world when he was in the depressed stage, he explained, to the extent that he became actually invisible. In this he reminds us a little of Grech, and we ventured to tell him so. Only a little, we hastened to add, he didn't have Grech's more egregious characteristics, not by any means. Who ever did? We'd first met him, Cliff, that is, not Grech, when we both fetched up at the Shell Beach Project, a little inland from here, when we were having our individual troubles, and Will, one of the workers, was instrumental in sorting them out. It is owing to his, Will's good offices, for instance, that we have the benefit of the nice blue tent here that one can zip up and be cosy within especially during the winter months. At that time, Cliff, temporarily homeless, made a very bad impression in the Project, but it was all a big misunderstanding and thanks to Will's patience it was cleared up and all was well in the end, and Cliff has a flat again now, obtained with the help of the Project, with the rent paid up to date, which we have seen and which is most acceptable. So that was how Cliff was fixed up. And Will the worker also then took us in hand, and led us into his office, to write down our details, so far as could be remembered. Name, he said first, and we were momentarily flummoxed. Colin Cloute, we affirmed, after a pause for thought, and he wrote that down on the form. We had been reading our Spenser, and recalled *"A shepheards boye, (no better doe him call,) / When Winters wastful spight was almost spent, / All in a sunneshine day, as did befall, / Led forth his flock, that had been long ypent"* (we were thinking of the gulls here, obviously). So that became the name by which we were known at the Shell Beach Project. And it went on from there. It was designed to form the beginning of a care plan, said Will. Going forward, he said – a formulation he liked, and repeated often. He prefers forward motion, does Will. That's what we're here for, he said, meaning the Project. People come to grief for all sorts of reasons, he said, usually not their own fault. We agreed. As previously stated, we have not recently been in a position to move forward. When one feels the pavement caressing one's cheek, it's not good, even if ever so briefly, it's not good, that. It's a bad sign. Nothing good can come of that. Will wrote all this down, and the tent was one outcome of this; it was furnished in time for the winter. We recall at this point that he also came to visit us more than once, kind Will the worker from the Shell Beach Project, to check our situation. And as it happened, he now visited again shortly after Mr Clifford Edgeworth had departed following his brief sojourn to research the gulls. Exit Unstable Cliff Edge, enter Will the Shell Beach Project worker.

He sat on the bench alongside, just as Cliff had done. A bright young man with a neatly trimmed beard and a light-weight Regatta jacket, for the weather was by now fairly clement, although the south-westerly breeze had started up again. Hello, mate, you all right? was his greeting. In response, we mentioned the business with the burgeoning building/unbuilding site, which was beginning to encroach on our area now, and to encroach further into our mind; the latest news being the garage and the line of redundant beach huts having been surrounded by new temporary security fencing, as we could both plainly see, and he nodded wisely, though without surprise; he evidently knew all this already, knew about the plans for *twenty-four holiday and family homes, comprising one- and two-bedroom flats and three-bedroom houses* on or right next to our manor. It's not great news, he said, you might find you'll be seriously inconvenienced at some point soon if you stay on here, and eventually, I am sorry to say, you will have to move on, but let's see. He had his clipboard and ballpoint pen out. He chatted amiably while we supped now and then from the thermos flask supplied by Sharonne (the Paisley pattern one today), and the time was spent pleasantly in this fashion. We observed meanwhile those few souls who passed by the shelter on their journeys up and down the beach path, most of them ignoring us. He continued to scribble on his clipboard pad. Well now, Colin, he concluded, I think we may have a viable plan for rehousing, if that is your wish, going forward. I'll leave you to your meditations. Do you call it meditation, what you do? And we replied that we didn't call it anything. In response to his inquiry, we outlined our experiments with thought, or our thought experiments, to put it another way. It's necessary to always break and regain symmetry, to not be trapped or have one's thoughts trapped in symmetry, we explained. So you have to turn your thoughts inside out, and only then can you really inspect them and find out what they're made of. And you discover that what you thought, that is, the construct built by your mind, was not necessarily true, was not necessarily apt and enlightening, but subject to constraints furnished by the hidden binaries that rule your mind without your knowing it, that is, below consciousness. But what do you mean, asked Will, by "turning your thoughts inside out"? We tried to answer him as best we could. How to use thought to question thought? We have been devoting a lot of time here on the bench to figuring that one out, we have been devising what one may term thought experiments. Yes, we said, some people do call it meditation; it's all right to call it that. The gulls do it all the time, we believe, but theirs are comparatively simple minds, they don't have dualistic concepts, they don't have ideas interfering and messing it all up, so their attitude to symmetry is plain, they don't ever think about it at all, either they are at one with their surroundings, in which case they are replete and they don't do much at all, or they are not, which is their experience of asymmetry, which means they have to feed or mate or follow whatever instruction the relevant part of their brain has issued, and then they do it, or if they can't do it they call, as has previously been described. They don't have any ideas. They have no idea what they are doing. Now, as to symmetry, we continued – seeing that Will apparently remained interested – no operation in the real world (so one reads in certain works of science and mathematics) will convert a right hand into a left without destruction. But we can convert a right glove into a left one by turning it inside out. Now this provides a clue. It furnishes us with a clue that may enable us to transform our consciousness, enable us to venture beyond the binaries that trap us, the left and the right and the black and the white and the red and the blue

and the male and the female of the species and the masculine as opposed to the feminine gender and the top and the
bottom and the south and the north and the east and the
west and the beginning and the end and the day and the
night and the light and the darkness and the here and the
over there and the before and after and the happy face and
the sad face and the major and the minor keys and the past
and the future (of course) and the interesting cases of pleasure and pain and heaven and earth or is it heaven and hell
and the positive and the negative and the Jekyll and Hyde
and the yin and yang; anyway, these binaries, dualities,
dichotomies, dyads, oppositions, polarities, contraries, all
of these we may transcend by means of a thought experi-
ment, whereby we make of our thought a glove, we might
imagine a rubber glove, blue in colour, though the colour
does not of course matter in the least as it is a mere thought-
glove, or alternatively imagined as a latex glove of a certain
degree of flexibility, such as we have encountered in
appointments of a medical or surgical nature, in settings of
that sort, for that is the quality we seek here, and if we have
been wearing this thought as a glove, well, we pull off this
thought-glove that we have been wearing so that it turns
completely inside out as it leaves our thought-hand, and
everything changes place, the yang and yin and the Hyde
and Jekyll and the negative and the positive and hell and
heaven and earth and heaven and pain and pleasure and the
future and the past and the minor and the major keys and
the sad face and the happy face and the after and before and
the over there and the here and the darkness and the light
and the end and the beginning and the west and the east
and the north and the south and the bottom and the top and
the feminine and the masculine gender and the female and
the male sex and the blue and the red and the white and the
black and the right and the left, and now everything is the

opposite way round and we have accomplished this without destruction, we have arrived at a new understanding, that is to say that these divisions are not all that there is and are by no means absolute, and we have arrived at an understanding of symmetry and how it might be broken.

The silence that followed – which was of course not silence at all, for it was filled with the soft whisper of the outgoing tide on the shingle, and the distant sound of the men's voices at the building site – was punctuated by Will the worker murmuring, Wow.

Finally, he got up as if to go.

Well, now – always nice talking with you, Colin. Is there anything else you'd like to tell me?

Yes, we replied, and it is this. The world we see is not reality itself but a projection onto our consciousness.

4 the sluice

Another day dawns, and it is the same as the day before. And the day before that. It's cold for the time of year. This is recorded in our notebooks. We write every day. We are persuaded that this clarifies our thought. But perhaps it would be better to dance. That's it. If one could dance, right here on the shingle, wouldn't that be something, wouldn't that be wonderful, wouldn't that be a sight to see, to tell one's children and grandchildren about, an old geezer dancing alone on the seashore, heedless of others, heedless of the effect on others, carefree or at least simulating carefreeness, that would be wonderful. It would be an example to others. It would be quite wonderful. But the bones and the sinews, alas, they are not up to it so much now. Oh come on, try it. It's all in the mind. It is forged in the mind. The dark things, and the trivial, and what washes and what won't wash and what washes away. All right, forget the dancing. Never mind. One could sing instead. That would be better, more feasible – or call, as the flock do, our friends the gulls again. They are still all around, attending to their business. Call and response – hope for response. Would there be a response? It might be a stupid one. People have always said stupid things. Give us a tune, they say. It has a tune, you can whistle it. But no-one whistles these days. No-one whistles now. Not even elderly gentlemen. So this solitary individual remains silent. What is this apparently inalienable entity known as an individual, anyway? A column of air in possession of a depository of memories.

Nothing more than that. And then what is to be done with this useless accumulation? Express it, that is to say get rid of it, traditionally that was by saying it in writing or out loud, and then you can start again. That was the original intention. So these thoughts come into my mind, said an individual once known as a poet – someone we once knew, could have been a poet, or maybe a philosopher, or a private investigator – and I have to write them down, just to get rid of them, he said, then I put them in a book, these thoughts in verbal form, but I end up not liking the book either, I end up wanting to get rid of the book too. That is a true story a poet told us.

A hundred metres or so to the west of our quarters – beyond the area where two or three small boats have been dragged up onto the beach amid an accumulation of fishing tackle – is a sluice that slowly disgorges into the sea. Or there may be. Of the various trips in that direction we may have made over a long period of time, a fair proportion do not result in the uncovering of such a feature. We draw a blank then. Perhaps on those occasions it has been overlooked; that no such sluice has been observed doesn't mean to say it doesn't exist, but rather is liable to be missed through not looking in the right direction at the right time. Yet on other occasions, there it is, unmistakably. Although the sluice may be mistaken. That is, it may be mistaken for a natural river, which it is not. When we say "disgorges into the sea" we may be misunderstood. In fact, the channel disgorged by the sluice, if it does exist, approaches the sea at well below the level of the beach, sur-rounded by steep embankments on either side, and disap-

pears into a tunnel beneath the beach, into caverns measure-
less to man, as the poet once said, or more prosaically into an
immense pipe or channel that plumbs the sea bed and may
be supposed to surface onto it some way from the shore,
there finally disgorging its contents into the murky water of
the deep. This excremental facility is what the sluice, whether
it appears to exist or not, is. What it happens to be. First it's
far away from perception, then it's in your face. That's the
way of it, that's what's meant by *is*. It is the channel that pre-
tends not to be. That may or may not be. But if you find it, on
those occasions you find that it's tranquil, its flow is sluggish,
almost still, it presents a greenish-brown surface, a silken finish, in its brief venture into the open air, and the embankment studded with ragged vegetation slopes down to it on
either side and holds it in place as it connects the bowels of
the earth to the bowels of the sea. On locating the sluice, it
may be observed that a path strays down one of the embankments to the side of it, a path that can be accessed by a broken
gate, half hidden at beach level; but can it really be accessed,
by which is meant, is access permitted or is it prohibited?
That there is a rather forbidding looking gate suggests the latter, but the gate is broken, which suggests that any implied
prohibition has been transgressed more than once – with
impunity, one may surmise. Certainly there isn't a notice displayed making prohibition explicit or warning of the dangers
inherent there. And so one time, on an occasion following the
first discovery, leaving the beach behind, we shouldered our
way past the gate and ventured with trepidation down there,
along the path that descends the embankment and levels off
to run parallel with the channel, which close up can be
observed to move no less sluggishly than it appears to do
from above, in fact hardly to move at all. Hardly. But it enters
the other senses here – well, we're talking about scent,
primarily if not exclusively. It smells. We smelt it. But it

doesn't smell as bad as might be feared; it's a kind of mustiness, the smell of old caves or old houses, and it was decided that this could be endured, in fact even enjoyed after a fashion, provided it didn't get any worse, didn't reach the point at which enjoyment tipped over that fine transitional line into disgust. The path continued alongside the channel; we followed it. Although this would have almost certainly been around spring, there was little sign of new life hereabouts. The broken vegetation that covered the embankment seemed ancient. No bees buzzed. Birds were absent. Our forward and downward motion was arrested only once: when suddenly noticing at our feet, laid demurely beside the path and half hidden by some dead bracken, the tiny corpse of a field mouse, belly-up, that had so far escaped the attention of predators. Its snowy belly and tan back marked it as *Apodemus sylvaticus* and distinguished it from *Mus musculus*, the common house mouse. Behind us, the dark water disappeared silently into the tunnel below the beach and the sea bed. It carried its human poison away into the depths. (This is why we shall never swim in that sea. We have observed many times the suds that appear on the waves, not a sign of health.) And then in the opposite direction, ahead of us, it emerged from under the steel girder railway bridge, a structure carrying the same line that passes behind our quarters. The path ran alongside the sluice and under the bridge, a ledge now at the side of the water, with the scent coming more strongly off it now. And then beyond the bridge the waterway vanished into cloacal darkness – the great hole in the earth that excreted it – and the path started to climb again to the lost daylight, veering rightwards. Here, on this first visit, at this point in time, there was a rapidly loudening thunderous noise: a train passing overhead. It was momentarily unbearable. There was a pause. So when that had finished, the climb commenced. The path led up to a lost patch of woodland, a mess of gnarled, stunted tree trunks and tangled bramble bushes. And everything started to come to life again. All around, wild garlic was found in abundance. Yes, it must have been the spring. Perching birds were heard here and there, secluded from the hegemonic rule of the herring gulls along the shoreline that had been left way behind; the mellifluous song of the blackbird was unmistakeable. It had Edenic qualities, this location. This world beyond the sluice. It seemed to belong to nobody, though there were glimpses here and there of security fencing or the remains of such that may have defended it from the outside world. The obscure birds clamour, as described by the lady in the play of course, we're just quoting from memory at this point; we do not have the book to point to, it's gone along with all the others, so we no longer have the means to pursue the reference. That would be the Scottish play. We marked this as a place where our thoughts might just be allowed to run free. And they did. There was the mellifluous blackbird again. And a rough, creaking noise, like the call of the raven himself. So we're found there in the midst of it, in the clothes we stand up, or lie down, in. We have no resources here, no buttress nor coign of vantage, but why, we could be free to smile and wave, bye bye, to sing, bye bye blackbird, observe a bloom of life that came out of nowhere, a cascade, with the looping birds and all of that activity. With their loops of song. We were in paradise, for a brief period. There are patches of sunlight on the broken ground. All life bleeds into other lives, as the nights and days do, that is, each bleed into each other, the invisible perching birds, the feathered fowl and the worms. Here the field mouse might face the owl's stare. A cascade of consciousness. We live with their shoulderblades, their skulls, we mark the fall of a tree. Here the world burns. We await the arrival of the swifts. But we remind ourself we have only the clothes we wear. And that this trip, as indeed every extended trip away from our normal quarters, including the daily visit to St Anthony's for ablutions, the occasional appointment at the Shell Beach Project and the infrequent patronage of the Angel public house, is fraught with danger, for everything else we may possess is always vulnerable if left. So on each subsequent visit, if we were to plan such, it might be expedient first to fill the capacious coat pockets as much as is practicable: but the books are too bulky, and must always be left in the tent, and the bedding and the changes of clothing likewise. The torch and the binoculars, they can be stuffed in the pockets, perhaps the flask, though admittedly that is not ours to remove *ad lib*. And certainly the notebooks, as many of them as will fit. But if so, if all of this is being so very seriously contemplated, why not go the whole hog, why not relocate here? Why not pitch the tent in the woods? Where there is more seclusion? We gave a lot of serious thought to this in the subsequent days and nights. And in particular on those darkest of nights within the tent when Sister Dream chooses to visit, rudely interrupting Sister Sleep, when the shakes visit, when useless memories take on new guises, when chimaeras and mandrakes crawl about in their own shit on endless staircases, when we wake to the continuous drilling of rain on the canvas overhead, when everything is louder than everything else, when above all of it Grech's coarse voice screams in our ears – those are the occasions on which such thought is triggered. The thought, specifically, to abandon the Council bench and shelter, to pack up the tent, heave all possessions onto the shoulders, to find the sluice again, and the woodland beyond it – that was the way the thought was tending. But then the counter-proposals, the objections, presented themselves in turn: that we would lose the good offices of Sharonne – her morning coffee, indifferent though it is, her personal kindness; that appointments with Will the outreach worker from the Shell

Beach Project would become more difficult; that Mr Clifford Edgeworth, variable as we find his company, would likely no longer arrive to pass the time of day from time to time; that morning ablutions would prove more difficult, St Anthony's then being considerably more distance away and more difficult of access, since it's clearly impossible to use the sluice for ablutions, much less for drinking water (though the option would be there to use it as a toilet, it being the final stage of a system of sewerage after all); that the sea that cannot be described and the flock of herring gulls that have almost become companions would be missed. All of these objections were raised. And then in turn some solutions presented themselves. With the acquisition of perhaps a small Calor gas stove, a kettle, a saucepan, well then, some rudimentary self-catering could be attempted, for instance. Sharonne's morning coffee could thus be replaced, and the current reliance on institutions for hot meals could even be eliminated. But then once again the counter-arguments arrange themselves: that acquiring extra possessions runs against our desire to free ourself of such as far as possible, to get rid of as much as possible in the interests of mobility and liberty (as of now, the entirety of the possessions, meagre though they are, poses a significant burden); and the further one, that suddenly occurs, namely that on the foreshore we are at least on public land, we are within our rights, whereas the sluice and the world that lies beyond it, while giving the appearance of nature, of an untrammelled wilderness, is very likely no such thing but is the property of a private authority, notwithstanding that there are no visible notices to that effect; and therefore camping on that land may well be considered trespass, and this knowledge represents the addition of an unwanted further burden. But also there is this to be considered: since our first discovery of this enclave we have been back more than once, and on half the occasions we have gained access and found it all as it was before, but on the other half of occasions we have passed the place where we thought the sluice was, and missed it completely, so that it would seem that its appearance is intermittent and not to be relied upon, and this puts us off. It puts us off considerably. It may be fair to say also that even those subsequent visits when we did succeed in locating it were never as promising as that first time when it had seemed like a veritable Eden, an ultimate refuge from the world at large; or to put it a different way, those subsequent visits did not live up to the promise of the first visit. But that disappointment aside, the possibility of not finding it at all would just put the tin lid on it. For suppose we did decide to do the thing, to move to the land beyond the sluice. We might have laboriously packed up all the belongings – the furled tent, the blankets, the cushions, the sleeping-bag, the towel, the spare clothing, the cagoule, the toilet requisites, the plastic cutlery, the torch, the binoculars, the broken phone, the money such as there is, the notebooks and pens, the library, not to mention Sharonne's thermos flask, or whichever of her flasks happened to be in our possession at the time, all of this carried in the rucksack and the holdall or in the capacious pockets – and with difficulty heaved them onto our person and sallied forth, only to subsequently discover that today the sluice was not after all to be found, and that we would therefore have to revert to the former position, our present station and quarters, though for all we know it might by that time have been claimed by another person in need, and we would then be in a greater pickle than before.

So far, so good. No, delete that. So far, so far. That's better
– more accurate.

Mr Clifford Edgeworth, while sitting on the bench alongside
during one afternoon of alternating cloud and sunshine, was
looking through our binoculars, which he, as is his wont, had
borrowed, at a tanker or some other vessel on the horizon. He
had started chattily but then became absorbed by his observation. For a while he was as still as he ever gets, though he's
never quite still but is always bobbing furtively. His hoodie
had been put on crooked, and he wriggled his scrawny neck
from time to time as though trying to escape from it. But then
he did settle into his observation properly, and a peaceful
silence came upon us, affording the opportunity for some
writing to be done. Even the gulls ceased their chatter for a
while. Finally, he put the binoculars down. Saw us scribbling
in one of the old notebooks: What are you writing, Phil, said
Cliff, what is it you're writing? This, we said, this is what
we're writing. What? This, just *this*, we explained. Ah, I see,
this. Then he paused for a long while as if to ponder, looked
around him, and came back with: Just this? Nothing more?
There are nuances to it, we explained. Our mouth, we
explained, must be imagined to be moving even as the reader
moves their eyes over these words. These words that are
being read now. He hesitated. I see, he said. That, we continued, that imagined movement might be an indication of
poetry, though not a guarantee of it. A necessary, though not
sufficient condition. I see, he repeated, nodding vigorously.
And then after another while he went back to his exploration
of the horizon while we continued our writing. He swept the

binoculars from side to side, rather too rapidly in our estima-
tion, back and forth across the never describable sea, and on
the rare occasions he held the instrument still his hands
trembled noticeably; it was a wonder he saw anything properly. He hummed something imperceptible, with gaps in
between the hums, while he was doing all this. Perhaps
extracts from his own compositions. Also, the impression
was given that he chuckled very softly to himself from time to
time – so that we momentarily feared for his mental health.
But he seemed in reasonably good spirits, there was probably
nothing to worry about, and we continued with our writing –
writing this, as always. Presently he put the binoculars down
again, nudged us, handed them to us, indicating we should
take a look. See that? We could not understand at first what
he wanted to draw attention to. There, on the horizon, there
are whole *cities* out there! he cried, look! What he actually
said was *whole fucking cities, it's fucking fantastic*, and he
repeated it more than once, dwelling on and revelling in the
fricatives and sibilants to the extent that he was spluttering
them liberally in our direction; had he been carrying the
plague he would have instantly transmitted it to us without
question. So we picked up the binoculars and trained them
on the horizon – while he exclaimed all the while: Can you
see? can you see? – and indeed the structure standing there
was awesome and intricate, a large vessel of some kind, full
of detail whose purpose was not apparent – we could only
speculate. What do you think that is, Phil? inquired Cliff
anxiously. That ain't a tanker! Asked for our opinion, we sur-
mised that it might be a large-structure-carrying vessel, but
he was not convinced. Are you crazy? he cried, snatching the
binoculars back to have another look himself, listen, that's no
ship, that's a fucking alien artefact, just look at it, that was
created by *no human hands*! We were reminded of his famous nickname, but forbore to mention this. A sea haze was

beginning to build up by now, and the outline of the supposed alien artefact was becoming more indistinct by the
minute until it was hard to make anything of it, though like
all other vessels it seemed to pass from left to right in accord-
ance with the rules of the shipping lane observable from this
point. And eventually it left our view and passed from our
consciousness, and Cliff began to calm down. We offered him
a custard cream from our little hoard, which he gratefully
accepted.

Do you ever think about Grech now, said Cliff suddenly,
munching on his second biscuit, do you ever think about
him? Who? we asked. Grech, he said, you keep mentioning
this Grech. No, not much these days, we responded, never
think of him from one dawn to the next dusk – though sometimes maybe from one dusk to the next dawn, then maybe,
then maybe then. Maybe then between dusk and dawn, but
no, never or rarely between dawn and dusk. But he is of no
consequence now, he is no longer alive. To all intents and
purposes. Ah, said Cliff. That's interesting, said Cliff after
another pause, between dusk and dawn he comes to you, but
not between dawn and dusk, there must be something significant in that, but I can't think what it is. And you say "to all
intents and purposes". Hmm. He paused again, waiting for a
response that was not furnished, was not forthcoming. So he
started once more: You never tell us what Grech was really
like, what was he like? There's not much to tell, we replied,
and besides he wasn't *like* anybody else, so it's hard to draw
comparisons that would make any sense. But you had a bust-
up, persisted Cliff, what was all that about, was it about this

girlfriend? No, not primarily, we said. The thing was this. Grech said something pretty ugly once, we said. And we have never forgotten it, for it was addressed to us, and got to the core of us. Grech himself was ugly, but in a pretty sort of way, in the way sin often is. That's how we remember him or the world remembers him in any case, but admittedly we haven't seen him for a while and memory can play false. We haven't cared to see him, that's all. He knew all about sin, for he was religious originally, or at any rate ostentatiously observed religious practices and outward signs, though of his inner nihilism, there is no doubt. We believe he was destined for the Church at one time, but he inclined towards the army. And after that, business. We try not to think about that, and we try not to think about Grech at all either; it suffices to say bridges were burned, nothing more was called for to be said, and nothing more *was* said, for a long time anyway, until he attempted a rapprochement, it would have been a couple of years later, two years after the thing he said, and by then we were having none of it so we turned away, we regret to say we turned away rejecting his proffered hand, with the ghost of a smile playing on our lips. Why? Cliff asked, his ears standing out all agog from the sides of his thin, dark face under his shock of white hair. Why? because we couldn't face him, we couldn't face up to what he was and, which was perhaps worse, what *we* were perceived to be, and whether that is what we were. And how long has it been? How long has it been since what? Since you last saw him, said Cliff, how long since you last saw Grech? Since we saw him, since he last spoke to us? Yes. About forty years, more maybe. Forgive us for rambling. It's turning out to be a lovely late afternoon, you have to admit, we said, attempting to change the subject, the clouds have begun to clear away and some late sunshine is poking through now at long last. Cliff acknowledged this. The grey-backed herring gulls and occasionally even terns were observed to flash by, necks outstretched; a flaxen-haired man trundled along the path past the bench on a mobility scooter, apparently asleep as he trundled. Look at that, exclaimed Cliff suddenly, pointing at the sea. Silvery mackerel flashed in and out of the water, for it was that time of year. Catch them unawares with a single outstretched hand: it's easier than getting a handle on this slippery world of lies, said Cliff, and we concurred. "World of Lies", that was one of his songs, we now recall. There were more and more people thronging the seafront now, even here, as if there were no plague circulating, as if there was everything to be confident about. Inside of us, we felt confident. Well, there is an infinitude of insides, granted, and the degree of confidence is infinitely variable as a result. But plagues pass. That one can say for certain. The beach will be thronging again, and then it will be deserted again, and we shall rejoice, in a way we have never quite managed in forty-some years. Winter will return, that's the best time – and Cliff agreed with this. You can see further inside your mind then, as far as is possible to see. The small kindnesses will surface then, one hopes, the brief smiles, the "All right, then?"s, the simple acknowledgements, the deviations from indifference, you can itemise them, sum them, so that they almost – do they? – balance the voids that inhabit the great void in which we all dwell. The very same void nonchalantly occupied by Grech, back then, in the time when he was unchallenged. (Ah! we're back to him, we cannot avoid it.) Nobody dared confront him at that time, though it was never clear why, what the dire consequence would be, for he was as mortal as any of us, that's for sure. Not that we knew then what would befall him, that he would die soon. So he *is* dead, then! said Cliff. Apparently – so it's said – but it isn't certain – he was said to have died not many miles from here, as it happens, just a few towns and fields away, presumably still unaware that deep within this world of appearances there is another world of appearances and another beneath that, and so on; no, he would never have attained that realisation, it would have been beyond him. He was a stupid man. That's not to say he didn't have a kind of cunning, enabling him to pinpoint instantly the vulnerable points in people and to home in on them without really understanding the nature of the vulnerability. Actually, he was a blank. He said many ugly things, unaware of their import, or their resonances far beyond the cloistered spaces in which he said them; it was fundamentally impossible for anyone, we suppose, to point this out to him, and it would have done no good at all, he would have laughed uncomprehendingly, the spittle from his laughter would have spattered their face, and the hysteria of his laughter would have spread to his friends, or shall we say his cronies, for he always had several, cronies, that is to say, not friends in the proper sense of course, those who hung on his words, such as they were, and repeated them to each other, giggling the while. But none of them, none of us, would have predicted his fate, or the series of events that precipitated it, over which we shall draw a veil, for it's not important: to relate them would confer an importance on Grech and his doings that he never merited in the slightest. One can speculate that he looked back on his life, from the loneliness and isolation in which he found himself in the nursing home to which he had been consigned, and felt some stirrings of remorse. (Which nursing home was that, then, didn't you say it was nearby? asked Cliff, but we ignored him and went on.) However, this would be to superimpose the glibness of hope onto the grim background of realism. Rather to the contrary, the brief reports that eventually filtered through to us were to the effect that he continued to his very last breath to laugh, to reminisce, to remember the "good old days", even to speak fondly of those he had abused back then, as though it had all been a game, the rules of which everyone had willingly adhered to in order for it to work its magic. They say he returned to the faith, and may even have received the last rites before he passed away, if indeed he did pass away – but these reports are not always to be believed. As to that ugly thing he told us, we've forgotten precisely what it was. You have to bear in mind that it was many decades ago. Pretty much all we remember, however, is what it meant, what it portended, the significance below the rough and inchoate shapes of his actual words, uttered spitefully and menacingly, even gigglingly, from a very close distance, and the rough and inchoate shapes of his mouth forming them. As we sat here on the beach, watching two herring gulls squabble over a fish-head or a chip wrapper, all of this came back to us, and will come back again, for certain. The sun was out now, and warming the deserted shingle. As we have previously observed, the beach is at times deserted, then fills with folk, then is deserted once more. But the thing that Grech said never manages to disappear, even if we can't quite remember its content. In summary, we told Cliff, the long and the short of it is that we carry it within us, and in this way Grech lives in us still. We were starting to drift off at this point. But I don't understand, Cliff suddenly said, digging us in the ribs – and we realised with a start he was now interrupting another incipient fugue, another invitation to the dance with Sister Sleep on the bench in the milky and evanescent sunlight, a stately and pleasant dance it promised to be – I don't understand, he exclaimed, is Grech dead or alive? We were now awake again. As far as we were concerned, we explained, he was dead and gone. But you remember, Cliff persisted, there was some doubt about that, you said, wasn't there some investigation, I think you said, about whether he'd really died? We cannot recall saying this, but may have done so in a reckless moment. There are an increasing number of reckless moments that cannot now be recalled. All that can be said is that if there was indeed an investigation and the results of it eventually became available, he, Cliff, would be the first to know. He replied that he appreciated that, but then asked to hear about Grech again, like a child requesting the repeat of a bedtime story – there were some details in our previous account that had puzzled him or that he didn't completely understand. What was his general appearance, Cliff wanted to know, there were some elements of our previous account that reminded him of somebody, and he wanted to check it wasn't the same person. Well, we explained, people sometimes said Grech was tall and gaunt but our recollection of him was different, more like squat and chunky. Ah, quite a difference, said Cliff, yes, quite a difference, but then memory does play remarkable tricks. Indeed, in some lights, we explained, people had even been known to confuse Grech with ourself. For example, a stranger had once greeted us as we were leaving a shop, then had broken off the greeting with an embarrassed: I'm sorry. Yes? I'm sorry, they repeated, I thought you were– But they did not need to say more, the fright first and then the sense of relief expressed in their eyes told its own story as they broke off the sentence. They did not need to complete it: *I thought you were Grech* was clearly what they meant, but they hesitated to offend us with this confusion of identities. But the rumours – that we were brothers, that we were twins, one rumour that spread was that we were once even conjoined – Conjoined? exclaimed Cliff, alarmed and puzzled, you mean, like Siamese twins? Yes, that we were joined physically, at the hip or at the shoulder or even the head – the details varied wildly. That's crazy, said Cliff, and we agreed. We agreed fervently. The very idea was hideous. Especially as Grech came from a privileged family, from a niche we had no access to. That ugly thing Grech told us all those years ago, making obvious the extent of his contempt, well, that wasn't really a surprise, it was just a distillation of what was already known. Everybody knew what he was, but few would say it openly, and none to his face. Especially as he grew more and more powerful. But in those early years, when we were students, all of that was dismissed as high jinks. Was that when you met your girl-friend? Cliff asked, you know, what was her name, Tabby something. Ah yes, Tabula Rasa, we recalled, we had forgotten about her. Tabula Rasa, that was the name we had dubbed her with, we had forgotten that temporarily. Tabula Rasa was in her prime then, alluring and sophisticated, though even then it was apparent this was something of an act, she was trying on mental costumes every day, and we fell for it. Everybody did. Everyone got drunk on the act, they wanted more of it, and the more she withheld the more they wanted. She was sharp at it, in the early days anyway, though things started to go to pieces later on. Much later on. But she was a leopardess, a vixen, a sphinx in her glory days. She was the Perfect Hostess, she was the It Girl of her generation. We fell under her spell, it has to be admitted. She had very high cheekbones, finely sculpted. She had high knees, and a sharp nose. In those days Grech was one of the duller ones, a plod-der, failed his exams repeatedly – one of his teachers is reputed to have told him at one time that if he worked non-stop for the next six months, putting aside all activities other than those aimed at passing the exam, he would only *just* fail – and it was known Tabula Rasa was openly contemptuous of him – but he always had an eye for the main chance. That eye was bleary, but had a cold gleam deep within it. How things changed. Did *she* change? When we first started living together, it at once became apparent that Tabula Rasa was not all she seemed – no, we correct ourself – actually, *seem-ing* was all she was, there was little more to her than the appearance she fostered, as we slowly discovered. There was a profound absence there. And what was more surprising was her neediness, something that was only manifested in private, and was an overwhelming drain on resources every single day, without let, in the way that she always wanted to draw us and anyone close, though there were not too many close to her, into her anxiety, to infect us with it and make us part of it. Are you fed up with me yet? she would say, which soon began to detract from her allure. And what about Grech during this time? Cliff inquired, having made polite "uh-huh, uh-huh" noises and nodded his head from time to time as we expounded. What about Grech? He was going from strength to strength. He had found he had a talent for business, by which we mean sharp practice, and he had fallen in with other talented businessmen, by which we mean crooks, and was beginning to prosper. Grech had actually evolved a personal philosophy, though he never referred to it as such, one in which the complexities of the world could be simplified and summed into opportunities on the one hand and threats on the other. And it followed therefore that the human race could be divided exactly, with no remainder: essentially, everyone was potentially either a victim or an enemy. The trick was to distinguish quickly between the two categories, and to act accordingly. This trick paid immense dividends to him. Grech, like Tabula Rasa, had no inner life that was worth taking the trouble to analyse, but he did learn, to give him his due, slowly and painstakingly he became an expert in simulating acceptable emotion, and that added to his store of capital. He could simper with the worst of them – are we boring you yet? – and many people would be taken in. He had never had either innate charm or intelligence, but now neither charm nor intelligence served any longer; they had been replaced by money, it was now money that did the heavy lifting,as they say these days. Now he had the Porsche he had always craved, he had two Porsches, he took flying lessons and bought himself a light aircraft. How could someone so fundamentally stupid as he was, more than one person remarked, succeed so brilliantly? Well, he did. He went into property, housing, medicine, whatever shook money out of the money tree. His speciality was buying up companies, exploiting their resources and selling them on just before they failed. It was thrilling, like ballet. Meanwhile, we had started our private investigation business, and also meanwhile the Tabula Rasa situation was starting to deteriorate: she was often drunk by now, tormented by what she always liked to call sentimentally her "inner demons", although as a matter of fact her interior was still an undiscovered country. As a matter of fact, one has to conclude, there was nothing there. So that ended badly. We shall say no more about it. Grech should have been in his pomp, but there were signs he was overreaching himself, the dance of money becoming ever more complicated, the show he put on, all glitter, resplendence, flash, a show in which cars, boats, private planes all figured, serving only now to mask the furtive moves behind the scenes, the diverting of funds from one company to another, for example the pension fund from one company providing the resources to pay off debts incurred elsewhere. In public, when he was seen, he was his usual arrogant self, but mostly he shunned the light; even at parties his absence was often remarked, sometimes he was discovered in a quiet room drinking heavily on his own. And rumours now reached us of the women he had paid off, but then also that the departed Tabula Rasa's new boyfriend was none other than Grech, which was said to be astounding, given the previous bad blood and mutual contempt, but when you think that Tabula Rasa was by then in dire need of money though still attractive, well, then, it was a marriage made in heaven, though it was actually made in Acapulco, so it was said. Well, many people lost out through Grech's business practices, and some were quite influential, and eventually we were persuaded by certain business associates to launch an investigation. And a great deal came out, including – but we did risk boring Cliff at this point, once or twice it was observed that he yawned, although this may just have been the effect of the sunshine – evidence of personal as well as financial transgressions, for instance that Tabula Rasa, who by then was rarely seen in public and on those few occasions was soberly dressed and grim-lipped, had been abused. But the case went on for years before Grech was convicted of a number of the financial transgressions he had been accused of, and fined very large sums of money. Upon which he filed a counter-suit for libel, which was successful, to our detriment. And so it went on. The upshot – no, it's too painful to recall. But hang on a minute, said Cliff, you said you last saw him forty years ago, but all these court cases and stuff, how old were you then, I mean you're a gentleman of advanced years now, but not as much as eighty or ninety, so ... We may have miscalculated, we conceded, we may have misrepresented the timeline. How did we start on all this anyway – ah yes, what Cliff may have been wondering about was that in later years the rumour went round that Grech had been reminiscing in the care home to which he had been consigned many years later about what he called "the good times" or "the good old days", though there was nothing good about them, and that he wanted to "bury the hatchet" – that was another phrase that leaked out – and it was even put about that we had agreed to go on a reconciliation mission with him. Reconciliation? With Grech? No way. No way, was our response. It was not possible, the very idea was obscene, it were better that his name be simply expunged from the record. As for getting to the bottom of this Grech business, of the Tabula Rasa business, well, it was too late for that now. It may be observed that this narrative lacks essential detail, or the details are contradictory, and there is no way to resolve those contradictions at this late point in time, but more to the point is the growing realisation over the years, and particularly during our sojourn here on the shoreline, that this *getting to the bottom* business is itself where it all goes wrong, because the fact is there's no bottom; everything is on the surface, everything is hiding in plain sight, there's no trick to it. Isn't that so? we appealed, but there was no reply, nothing was coming back now, and quickly we realised Cliff was no longer there, had probably by now gone home (when had that been?), and only the remnant of discourse was left, the remnant of what was no more than inconsequential babbling beside the vastness of the sea, which was tranquil as far as the eye could make out. Immensely tranquil. And another evening was coming on: the sun was now pink on the horizon, having descended behind a low shallow bank of grey cloud only to reappear briefly just prior to its extinction. So far, so far. The sea was empty. That is to say, empty of floating craft, there being no sign on the surface of the life that would always be teeming in its depths for all we knew. But that life did not concern us. Certainly there was no sign on the horizon of the structure Cliff had fancifully suggested might be an alien city; no, the alleged city had gone, vanished without trace. Has it previously been mentioned that the horizon today had a hard edge?

Mr Clifford Edgeworth must have taken his leave, then, though we have no recollection of it, and we were left to contemplate the coming evening, to consider the possibility of a pleasant walk up the beach, certainly not as far as the sluice, but a little way along, to see what could be found among the debris left by the receding tide, not to mention finding a place to piss, before returning to the sandwich that had been secreted within the tent earlier, and to a continuation of reading by torchlight, to sorting through the patchy depository of memories before bedtime. But we had seen the best of the day, and that was brief enough. It had peaked momentarily, and now the future returned to haunt us. The flock were beginning to get restless, as though they knew – in their wisdom, which they are totally unaware of because fundamentally stupid – that something was up, as though they knew the end was coming, would have to come. One was whimpering incessantly. And then they started the quarking, one started, then others copied it, the whole thing spread among the flock far and wide, the quarking started, and went on for some while.

5 are you in the fucking zoo

There seemed to be an intrinsic luminosity to everything that was, and everything it would become. The seashore: there it always was and there it always will be – it will outlast us, of course. The luminosity coming and going, of course. The same proportion of light to darkness when averaged out over the year, every year, but the daily proportions of course varying, for we are in the northern hemisphere, and just now the quantity of light increasing in proportion to the hours of darkness, but after the summer solstice of course beginning to tend to quite other. It's the saddest day of the year. But that's the way it heaves and slumps. That's how it always was. So far, so far. Because it was, is that all it will become? Something is always happening. What it essentially was lay elsewhere. It was enough to be born, without this. Without this, what do you call it, *imbroglio*. A word we are pleased with, and which we repeat. We have no truck with *imbroglio*. In all its shapes and forms. Nothing becomes but what will be. And our wants were modest, after all. A place to be undisturbed in. Somewhere to think our thoughts, somewhere to do our humming. It could be a cathedral or a pigsty, it makes no difference. There has been a lack of understanding about this. That is what we were thinking. About what there was and what there will be. About the objects people left behind. You could see a bird in the rusty streaks, or a beast, or any shape you wanted to. You could see a bird that wanted to fly from the concrete in which it was embedded. That wanted to but could not. Any shape you wanted to see you saw. Everywhere, birds were embedded in the rocks, in the concrete, everywhere you looked. Then when you looked again, they were gone. A hobgoblin, shrouded. It was there, it was near the seashore. One of the flock, a cock on his dunghill crowing. It was there, but it was out of focus. Some sticks, what did they mean. An awesome Buddha in the rocks. It wasn't moving. It will not move. The young ones had been kicked out of the nest, and though they pleaded and whinged there was nothing doing. A ruffian dog moved about the place, searching, for what. Mischief light on him. A dog with flesh in his mouth. No sooner was he out but that, swifter than thought, all was devoured. We are at rest. We have left the world. So far, so far. After a while, the words seemed to march across the page by themselves. See what it's like when you aren't here. A dog, but it was out of focus. Everything was out of focus. The rust marks and streaks on the concrete, the stains that had suggested beings and wraiths and creations of all kinds, but that on further scanning had been revealed to be no more than the action of oxygen and water on ferrous materials bleeding onto the walls, onto the rocks, onto the beach as far as could be seen. The beach was scanned. A single flip-flop, dirty pink, was found. Also part of a trainer. Several crumpled beer cans. Several plastic bottles, of assorted provenance. Fragments of expanded polystyrene, imitating rock. Rubber fragments were also found. A child's plastic cricket bat. A pair of sunglasses, the left lens missing. An intact scallop shell. Several plastic bags and fragments of bags, some with miscellaneous content. Beer bottles. They reeked. On the shingle, dotted around, for there is little sand here. Disposable diningware. A blue soiled rag that turned out to be a child's T-shirt. Sadness collected within us. A mermaid's purse was found. Parts of an umbrella. The almost intact skull and ribs of a skate. Chocolate wrappers, empty sweet bags. Miscellaneous slender cylinders. The delicate skull of a herring gull chick. A half-eaten sandwich, contents unknown. Chip wrappers. All were present. They were all visibly present, though all out of focus.

The *contretemps* with the foreman of the works – which we had been dreading for some days now, having observed him scouting round his site, casting lowering glances in our direction every now and then, glances we and he both avoided as soon as they were registered – finally took place, as it happens, while Will was present and able to witness the encounter. It was one of his, Will's, weekly pastoral visits. We always saw Will approach from afar, from the east, bearing gifts, and in contrast to the dance with the foreman we would instantly acknowledge him and he would wave cheerily even as he approached. Will the worker from the Shell Beach Project, bless him, had taken to regularly bringing us a six-pack of plastic bottled water, for the purpose of hydration. Here you are, Colin, he'd say each time. Nice to see you looking so well, Colin. Hydration had become very important to him recently. He lectured about it from time to time. His nature is benign, he is doing his best, and it is necessary to acknowledge that. We accepted the bottles with good grace, and they were ranged about us, both in the tent and outside the tent, but it was more than we could do to keep up with it all. And where to dispose of them, if and when used? Ah. A whole new set of problems. But then, an emptied bottle, employed perhaps within the tent in the middle of the night, when the urge came suddenly, rudely interrupting Sister Sleep, to urinate ... why not avoid going out into the cold, in the dark – pee into the empty bottle instead, why not, then at leisure it could be disposed of in the morning, at dawn, by pouring into the rolling waves. But this turned out not to be practicable on account of the mouths of the bottles being too narrow, it was not possible to achieve the necessary accuracy, especially in the dark, and so this solution became worse than the problem. Forget that. It would have given us a new problem, one with implications of hygiene management. But leaving the relatively warm environment of the tent at night is always a trial, especially when the wind is presenting itself, *when the westerly is blowing sore*. So, be that as it may, Will approached once more, with this week's six-pack of water, with the cheery wave: Hi Colin, how you doing? But no sooner had he got here this time than the foreman was with us. There was no wave from the foreman. His approach was rapid: one moment he was over at the building site, the next he was in our faces. How it was done we did not know, we had not observed, distracted as we were by the approach of Will from the other direction. In our faces all of a sudden, and his own a ratlike face, the adjective being summoned to mind because of the face's narrowness and the prominence of the incisors between his thin lips – come to think of it, a ratlike demeanour and body too, built for weaving and squirming, for suddenly darting hither and thither unpredictably. It made the heart jump. And so there were three of us ranged around the bench, him in his hard hat and hi-vis jacket, Will in his Regatta jacket, ourself in the favoured overcoat. Excuse me, he said, to Will, not to ourself, Excuse me. Is this gentleman moving on, then? I beg your pardon? replied Will sweetly, a winning smile on his face. This gentleman, said the foreman – he indicated our presence with a curt flick of the palm in our direction – is he going to be moving soon? Ah, said Will, let me introduce you, this gentleman is Mr Colin Cloute, and my name is Will, I work at the Shell Beach Project, who are we speaking to, may I ask? The foreman did not volunteer his name, but grunted. Only, I'm in charge of the building works that are shortly to be taking place here, he said, so we need to secure the area, like, now please. Hold your horses, says Will, Mr Cloute is aware of the pending building works, and we are talking about a care plan that will enable him to vacate the area in good time for them. I know for a fact they are not due to start for a few weeks yet. We need to secure the area, repeated the foreman of the works, just letting you know. And with that he turned and went back to the site. So Will and ourself were left looking at each other. Arsehole, said Will, and there was laughter. We should not worry, said Will, we should persevere with our plan. He sat down on the bench. Lovely day, innit?

Gentleman, the foreman had said, sarcastically. We had heard that before, of course. Come away from that gentleman! The cry echoed from the rocks and the chain-link fencing. On that occasion it was a woman's voice, a confident, commanding voice. Her child was sombre, chubby-cheeked, with mournful dark eyes that could be induced to brighten if one smiled at her, with dark brown hair falling asymmetrically onto her blue anorak. She stood still, staring at us, hands on the handlebars of her miniature pink bicycle. Come away from that gentleman, darling, the mother ordered, in her authoritative voice with an edge of concern. But the voice was dislocated from her body. Her eyes were elsewhere, she was out of reach, indescribable. Her hair was blonde-streaked and she wore her sunglasses on the top of it. *Come away from that gentleman* – yes, words of solicitude on the face of it, as if being scrupulously polite, as if intending to be protective of our privacy, but even as the words were being emitted – you might say spat out – and especially while the emphasised phrase "*that gentleman*" was being articulated, her body language was at the very same time explicitly denying our presence, that is to say, like the foreman, she pointedly didn't look in our direction while speaking these words that clearly referred to us, she looked in every direction but, so it was made to seem that "that gentleman" was a terrible void she couldn't bear looking into, a void she was urging her child to move rapidly away from. And reluctantly, it seemed, under her guidance the child turned her pink bike around, turned away from the void and, her little feet starting to pump the pedals, headed back into her world.

Angus and Queenie visited once or twice during the period being documented here, in passing on their way to the Angel, which we no longer frequent, for reasons given above. It is their gait that first announces their oncoming presence: Angus a constant shamble, constant that is in velocity (slow) if not in accuracy of navigation, for he wavers as he comes, even though presently sober, and also has a regular list to one side; and Queenie with birdlike movements at his left flank, that is to say quick and jerky – and they start hailing us from afar, while they are still on the path from the west, from their home *en route* to the Angel. Hey Phil, said Angus said Queenie, in their florid way, how are you doing, as they came into earshot, as they came up to us and plumped themselves down on the bench next to us; not bad, we replied, not bad, thank you. You coming for a drink, Phil? no, no drinking, we don't do the drinking any more, we said (we don't have the funds, we don't say, we are fearful, alas, for our possessions left here on the foreshore, we don't say). You being rehoused, Phil? chirruped Queenie, we heard you was being rehoused. Where did you hear that? Oh, said Queenie mysteriously, the grapevine, you know. *I heard it on the grapevine*, Angus immediately began chanting, *Not much longer would you be mine...* Well, this particular grapevine, we suggested, may not be the most accurate conveyor of information; if we are moving from here there's a long way to go. And now on this occasion we were joined unobtrusively by Mr Clifford Edgeworth, who had sidled up and entered the conversation without seeming to do so. Where had he come from? Undoubtedly from his home, the flat in which he himself had been resettled. Cliff had ideas of his own, as always. And so the conversation between the four of us centred on the notions of moving on and resettling and what forms these might take, though Angus continued to sing obsessively under his breath from time to time (*Not much longer would you be mah baby* ...) during the lapses in discourse. These topics occupied us all while the waves lapped in the distance, while the ominous continuing activity in the building site could be observed and could not be ignored. But after a while Angus and Queenie, having failed to persuade us to join them in their present quest for refreshment, stood up, bade their farewells and continued on their way, probably to the Angel. Almost certainly to the Angel. Cliff demurred, on the grounds that "it's too early for me". So he now took his place on the bench alongside us (the same place just vacated by the pair), having been standing patiently for a while. He had shown signs recently of wanting to spend more time in our vicinity; he had taken a shine to it (the vicinity) and to us, and his visits were becoming now both more frequent and more prolonged. Unstable Cliff Edge, always listening to absent musics that present themselves inside his brain, always in the centre of it all, had come today expressly to show us footage on his hand-held device of himself in his pomp all those years ago, footage he had promised to show on his previous visit. The video depicted him performing with his band at a high degree of mania, his almost unrecognisable younger self like an animated skeleton in a training video, deploying his sun-burst Fender guitar as if it were a sub-machine gun, the other Suckling Rats around him as he weaved, advanced and retreated, alternately nodding his head and turning his back, ignoring the expression of utter dementia in the staring eyes of his bandmate the vocalist who waved the microphone stand perilously in the air, while the drummer, naked to the waist, grinned broadly as he thrashed, and the bass player (Shammy Leather, we recall) remained a soldierly statue, grim-faced, portending mock evil. The sound quality on his device was poor, for which he apologised more than once: the treble tinny, we noted, the bass artificially boosted, and not much in between. We were so *young*, he commented mourn-fully as he contemplated the jerky images held in his palm, with the reverence some confer on religious icons. What planet were we on, he continued, murmuring now as he con-templated, calmed by the objectivity of time passed. What fucking planet? But the sun was now reaching its apogee above the that part of the planet we were both inhabiting in the here and now, and we were looking forward to and indeed longing so for a brief and peaceful dalliance with Sis-ter Sleep, here on the very bench in the sunlight, so that after a while we struggled to make sense of his discourse. And things became pleasantly discombobulated in our head as the benevolent sister's influence slowly overcame us, so that we nodded off. When consciousness was regained, it may have been half an hour or more later, Cliff was now found to have moved on: in spirit that is to say, he was still here physically beside us on the bench but he had put away his device and again picked up our binoculars which usually rested on the bench during the hours of daylight, and was once more scanning the horizon from side to side as is his wont. When he saw our eyes re-open, he violently nudged us. Phil, Phil! he cried in great excitement, trembling, trying to hand over the binoculars. For some time now he had been obsessive about the distant structures he observed that appeared from time to time out at sea, fantastically complicated and extensive, though too far off for him to discern details, even with the help of the borrowed binoculars. He had previously discounted our explanation that those features were components of an oil rig, perhaps, being towed from its place of manufacture to its destined location. There it is again, Phil! he exclaimed hoarsely. Come on! Fuck me, what *is* that! So he thrust the binoculars into our hand and it is the case that through them a complex of gunmetal shapes could be observed once more, stood on the hard edge of the horizon, apparently unmoving. Immensely complicated structures: towers, pipes, ducts. It wasn't possible to focus on any detail for very long. A rig of some sort. No, no, he exclaimed, seizing back the binoculars, you keep saying that, Phil, no, a city. That's what it is. An alien city. And he wouldn't be budged on this. The same city, reappearing again and again, we asked, or a different city each time? He thought for only a moment. Oh, the same one. Definitely the same one. So where is it on those occasions, that is to say most of the time, when it can't be seen on the horizon (in this, it occurred to us, it resembles the area of the sluice, which appears at some times and not at others)? Here, Cliff had to think a little longer, searching his mind for a solution that would preserve the appearances and suit his narrative. On the sea floor, he suggested. Like a vast analogue of Jules Verne's *Nautilus*, this mobile city would traverse the oceans, surfacing on occasion, for what purpose he would not

or could not say, and it was clearly populated by marine intelligences, he continued, warming to his theme now, heedless
of the need to provide evidence and relying solely on the force
of his imagination to generate plausible or not so plausible
explanations; intelligent marine beings, he suggested, probably not cetaceans such as dolphins and whales, but beings
that were capable of constructing artefacts and perhaps even
of existing for short periods out of the water, in all probability
therefore cephalopods, yes very likely, that is to say creatures
of the family of the octopus, the squid, the cuttlefish and the
chambered nautilus, which are said to possess high intelligence and advanced organising capabilities even among the
species already known to us (and do you know, it's dispersed
intelligence, half of their brains are in their arms!), and
moreover are capable with their tentacles of manipulating
objects and therefore potentially of constructing complex
forms. Who knows, he exclaimed, in the depths of the ocean
that humanity has not yet explored, that is more a mystery to
us even than the deserts of Mars, who knows what highly
evolved beings may have developed among the class of *Ceph-
alopoda* over millions of years? We paraphrase his discourse;
the exact form of his words we struggle to reproduce. In
Cliff's theory, elements of which were clearly being developed
on the fly, there has been more than ample time in the five
hundred or so million years since the Cambrian explosion for
a species to evolve deep on the ocean floor, eventually attain-
ing the ability to construct complex habitations, indeed cities, that are capable of moving from place to place and even
on rare occasion, as now before us for example, to rise to the
surface for what purpose we can only speculate, perhaps to
scout out new territories, new possibilities for their species to
take advantage of, and if so arguably pose an actual threat –
wait a minute, we intervened, a threat? what kind of a threat
are you now envisaging? – a threat to our way of life, he con-

tinued nonchalantly, enjoying the rush he was now on, a threat to the *whole of fucking humanity*, he repeated, his voice now raised and a fleck of saliva at the corner of his thin lips, which were nevertheless smiling throughout, showing crooked teeth, so it was impossible to get a sense of where he actually stood on all this wild and wonderful speculation. He paused, and cleared his throat noisily. Stranger things have happened, he said, defensively now. Not too many, we suggested. In fact, hardly any at all. Come on! said Cliff, it's plausible, you've got to admit it. No, it's as far from plausible as you can get, we contended, but he wasn't listening. Nature is wonderful, he insisted, anything can happen, and anything that can happen *will* happen, somewhere in the universe, you know what I mean? They now think life is prolific everywhere in the universe. They do? Oh yes, he said, there's thousands of exo-planets been discovered round distant stars. For example, there is a planet where it rains iron, did you know that? he demanded – so anyway, they've now discovered exo-planets, he said, where all these things happen that we just can't conceive of. But we are not on an exo-planet, we are on planet Earth, we reminded him. Well, he said, delivering the clincher, his small keen eyes gleaming lustrously, to anyone on the other side of the universe we *are* an exo-planet. He let that sink in. And like I said, he continued, we know less about what goes on in the oceans than we know about Mars, let alone any exo-planet. Who knows how long the octopus people – that's what he started calling them – have been evolving? Who knows indeed? Who knows anything? That, we admitted, was the big question. Who knows anything? It was, we suggested, something always to bear in mind. Our advice on such questions is generally considered and disinterested. And during all these exchanges, and during the brief silence that followed them, the gulls started to become restless again, while still the mysterious structure stood on the horizon, though there was never any sign of life on them, and certainly not of the super-molluscs of Mr Clifford Edge-worth's imagining.

It was as that evening came on (and its incidence was notice-ably later now as the northern hemisphere continued to turn from the solstice – but still the fading of luminosity was inex-orable), that the intruders were perceived. It was what we had dreaded for so long. That they were instantly designated as "intruders" rather than categorised with the other casual passers-by that one would expect in this area of the shoreline every day and even at this late time of day was attributable not so much to their appearance as to their body language: their gestures, the way they carried themselves, the way they interacted physically among themselves and with the envir-onment. There were two of them. They were young, and male. But they were not visually present at first. It was a while before they presented themselves. It was not their appear-ance that first impinged upon our consciousness; it was sound that announced them. Or a succession of sounds. The first, out of nowhere, which startled us, was a clanging that reverberated from afar, a single sound event as it seemed at first; but after a short interval it was followed by another, and thereafter by repeated clangings at irregular intervals, each one sounding inexorably nearer and louder. This was not normal; this was worrying. And then the clangings were interspersed with shouting: a shout and a clang, then a clang and a shout. Eventually, they began to show themselves, approaching along the pathway from the east: two youths, long-shadowed, each deploying what appeared to be the remains of a deckchair to attack the chain-link fencing repeatedly, in some insane competition, and each time they had done so they were moved to giggle and shriek and swear, in a spirit of triumph. So the planet turned and the boys advanced. By the time they got close, though, they had already tired of their game and each in turn threw the dismembered deckchair components onto the shingle, as though shedding parts of themselves. And now they revealed themselves as they were, unencumbered. More boys than youths, in fact. Children, even. But menacing ones. White. They were roughly identical but of slightly different sizes. Their hair was dense with gel, their trousers sagged and bagged like elephant legs. Both wore hoodies with the hoods down, one black one pale grey. There was a family resemblance in their thin faces. They stopped when they saw us and our quarters. They grinned with their faces, but their eyes were dead, like those of baby lemon sharks weaving their way through mangrove shallows – though sharks do not of course strictly grin, their mouths being turned down, not up, at the sides. This was uncanny. Even Grech at his worst was not so coarse. After a while, the taller and probably older of the two shouted: Hey mister, give us a drink! He was pointing at the stack of plastic water bottles next to the tent. Our silent nod and gesture was intended to convey that they should help themselves and then move on. The older boy ran up, seized a six-pack, ripped the polythene wrapper and extracted a bottle; removed the cap, which he flung onto the shingle, put the bottle to his lips, gulped, removed it from his lips, then, holding it in both hands, with a shout jerked it repeatedly in the direction of his companion, spraying him (like a Grand Prix winner celebrating), then discarded the bottle on the shingle. The companion screeched with mixed outrage and delight, picked up the bottle from the shingle, flung it back at the first one, then himself ran up to us, seized another bottle from the torn polythene, ripped off the cap in exactly the same way the first had done, upturned it over his head and showered himself with water. Ha ha, shouted the bigger one. There followed a water fight, half on the path, half on the shingle, the boys alternately picking up one of the bottles and shying it at each other. We watched all this from our bench. Finally the bigger one turned and threw his bottle, spraying the last of its contents, deliberately against our tent. We tried to catch his darting eye; we said quietly, with what composure and force could be mustered: Please don't do that. The boy found this exceedingly funny. *Please don't do that!* – without looking in our direction, he repeated our words to his companion in an extreme parody of our intonation, who replied by repeating the same words back, in a strangulated tone that both immediately found humorous. They laughed with their dead eyes for a while. Then they didn't know what to do next. They stared in our direction; we gazed out to sea. The bigger boy shouted: What you doing here? We made no reply. What you doing here? Looking at the sea, we said. He's looking at the sea, did you hear that? They seemed to think this was hilarious. Why you here? demanded the smaller boy. We made no reply. Why you here? Why you here? Why are *you two* here? we asked in return. Did you ever think of that? They were nonplussed. They could not think how to progress the conversation. At last the bigger one said: You're not supposed to be here. Why not? we asked. It's against the law, innit? he ventured. What law? *The law*, he insisted, don't you even know the law, your sort of people ain't supposed to be here. We made no reply. Nobody wants your sort of people here! The smaller one laughed in approval. Are you two brothers? we asked politely. That ain't nothing to do with you, said the bigger boy. Have you nothing better to do? we asked. The boy stared at us. Fuck off! he said, and the smaller, perhaps his younger brother, laughed again at the witticism. But by now, they were becoming bored again. They had started to move off. Then the bigger one turned and from a safe distance shouted again: Fuck off! This is *our* beach! Fuck off from our beach, fucking scum, fucking homeless scum! With that, they turned and ran away westward down the path, giggling the while, until they disappeared from sight and sound.

Within the warm dark cuddle of the tent, as Sister Sleep was being beckoned once more, from out of nowhere a strident if slightly muffled tone suddenly interrupted the silence. This had never happened before. A five-note motif, repeated over and over, a harsh digital approximation of a blues lick, played by no human hand, the emanation of a phantom keyboard pounded by an unearthly intelligence. It would not let up. Over and over. But if it had never happened before why was it so ominously familiar? Where was this repetitive sound coming from? Investigation showed it to be louder in the vicinity of the rucksack in which various possessions not presently being used were being stored, and soon enough the answer to the riddle was provided. It was none other than our mobile phone, dead for over a year, its SIM card presumed missing or defective, and besides lacking the means to refresh its electricity supply, yet now ringing urgently, querulously, without let, and, once uncovered, without the muffling. Outside the tent meanwhile the bickering of the gulls could be heard starting up again: there clearly had been an issue to be dealt with. We picked up the phone, pressed the button, held it to our ear. A voice came on the line, a terribly familiar voice, condensed out of the air within the tent.

It called our name. *It called our name.* We answered it, with immense trepidation. Where are you? the voice demanded, where the fuck are you? We remained silent. The line crackled slightly. The gulls could still be heard outside the tent, squabbling. It was clear now who this was, there could be no doubt at all. *Where the fuck are you?* What's that I can hear? Are you in the fucking *zoo?*

There was no doubting whose the voice was. It was the voice of Grech. It was Grech on the line, as full of menace as ever, just as though he had never been dead.

6 down the rabbit hole

ehind a tall gingham curtain along the left-hand side of a long corridor leading to the toilet were revealed row upon row of wooden shelves, floor to ceiling, on which were stored objects upon objects. The boy saw in the dim light, high above him, too high for him to reach, old-fashioned leather suitcases. Further down, stacks of neatly folded fabrics: sheets, blankets, more curtain material. Umbrellas. An old Bakelite telephone, black, with a heavy metal dial. Some ancient mechanical objects of mysterious function. A golfing bag, stacked on its side, the heads of the clubs within showing. Two wooden tennis rackets. Cardboard boxes, some of battered appearance, which he managed to pull halfway out to inspect: they were Scrabble, Cluedo, Monopoly, other board games of various sorts. He recognised these games. A chessboard. Stray chessmen seemed to have walked free of their box and now patrolled the shelves individually. There were wonderful model locomotives in repose, which he didn't dare touch. China dolls of different sizes, their limbs held out stiffly, their blue glass eyes staring malevolently at nothing. Pots and pans, real ones and toy ones. A kettle of an antique design, without the lid, revealing a furred interior. Large books stacked side by side: revealed when pulled out to be children's annuals of a generation past: *Tiger Tim, Teddy Tail, Rupert Bear,* their colourful covers battered, evidence of loving attention. The boy picked out one of these annuals. He looked round him once again. Nobody there. He continued along the corridor towards the toilet, which had been his objective, with the book under his arm. He pulled open the door and entered the toilet, pulled close the door and secured it with the latch. There, hidden away from everybody else, in seclusion on the wooden toilet seat, he opened the book on his lap and began to read. He read stories and gazed at pictures of tigers and mice and rabbits in breeches and boots, and pretty soon he was transported into another world. Was it minutes or was it hours that went by? But inevitably he began to hear faint calls. He heard his name being called. He was being called to come for his tea. What happened next? It isn't at all clear. The boy has vanished.

There is nothing now but blue light flooding consciousness. It comes out of nowhere and is everywhere. We are in the middle of everywhere. Isolated calls may be heard coming from somewhere, monosyllabic, keening. Someone or some creature is calling. Everything is vibrating. The light is accompanied by an increase in temperature. It has become moderately hot. The blue material above and all around has a distinctive odour. The calls receive an answer. It must be morning. It will be a warm day. The tent material is warming up. Gulls are conversing. The sound of waves can be heard in the distance. Everything vibrates constantly.

A dim corridor, just some light from a window at the far end, a gingham curtain covering the whole of the left-hand wall, concealing various dream objects from the past, on stacks and stacks of shelves. Like a dream – because dreams are invariably poorly lit. We discern that a small boy approached with creaking footsteps, and with trepidation parted the curtain. The boy, our protagonist in this narrative, was slight, slender-boned, you might say puny, with a constantly puzzled expression, in short dark trousers and a white shirt, his feet in slippers. He was looking for books, children's annuals of previous generations that he had seen before, to take down and read in seclusion, perhaps in the toilet at the end of the corridor. He selected one, depicting a friendly, clothed bear leaping on a hillside, whose promised adventures seemed to provide an opportunity for absorption. The bear, who was brown and wore brown boots on the cover, but in an inexplicable shift of identity became white with white boots inside the book, was transported by a dragon to a magic island, or to a sorcerer's castle. He only ever wanted to do good, but somehow things always got out of hand. In this world, animals with human bodies and wearing human clothes predominated, and spoke dialogue, but sometimes real humans and real animals appeared, not to mention eloquent elves. The real animals rarely spoke. And so he took the book to the toilet, and returned it, and next day he was back again. He noticed there was a row of other books, on a higher shelf, darker and smaller ones, scented faintly but pleasantly with mustiness, as he found when they were taken down, which was done with great difficulty. This was only a boy with a boy's body, after all. He held the books, which were dense with type, which rarely included pictures, but which intrigued him. He thought about where he might go to read them, to the toilet again perhaps, or else the room with the piano. Could he dare go there? It would be more comfortable.

Yes, perhaps the room with the piano today. A couple of the books under his arm, our protagonist turned round and retreated towards the door by which he had entered, found another door, entered the room that smelt of furniture polish, the room with the piano. On the dark upright piano, whose lid was closed, stood a framed photograph, a black and white portrait of a man and a lady in formal clothes, unsmiling. It was a still afternoon, with the fine dust motes lazily drifting in the beam of sunlight that penetrated from the window beyond the piano; there was nobody about. The boy settled down in the florally patterned armchair, opened a book and was immediately absorbed. A clock ticked loudly in the room. Where are these events taking place? The boy was sprawling in the armchair, reading, lost to the world. Was he really a boy with a boy's body? he was, but where was he, in the corridor, in the toilet, in the room with the piano, or in a bleak place overgrown with nettles which was the churchyard, and beyond which was a dark flat wilderness, intersected with dykes and mounds and gates? And were his parents really dead and buried here? Was his name unpronounceable, or was it really Pip? All stories exist simultaneously. And now it seemed to him that he was upside down, his pockets emptied, and he saw the church steeple under his feet. Or was he falling headfirst down what seemed to be a very deep well, and was he now a girl and was his name now Alice? Was he falling very slowly, and were the sides of the well filled with cupboards and bookshelves, with maps and pictures hung upon pegs? Yes he was. Other creatures appeared. There was a mouse who told his tale. There was confusion about whether it was a tale or a tail, and it dwindled away surprisingly. This was alarming as well as confusing. More doors leading to doors. And to doors after that. The farther door of this room, which has not previously existed in this narrative, opened, and in came a mature lady of dark and unfathomable complexion who bore an immediately identifiable resemblance to the lady in the photograph on the piano. She was wearing a floral dress that nearly matched the floral armchair. She was robustly made, with a slight dewlap at her throat, and dark, piercing eyes that could be discomfiting. But she now contemplated the child with emotion. She said: Oh, my poor, poor boy! The boy was startled. You found the books! she exclaimed. He stood up from the armchair, dropping the book he'd been reading. He shifted uncomfortably. Suddenly he was enveloped in his aunt's considerable embrace, a fit of emotion having overwhelmed her. He observed silently, and without understanding, that she had changed her tune. Far from reprimanding him, as he'd expected, she was now showing unrestrained and frankly alarming love. You poor boy! she continued to exclaim. It's all right! He was confused because the first time they'd met, when he was in his new coat, in a new country, hers had been an astringent welcome. You are coming to live with Uncle and me, she had told him. Now the first thing you must know is that I run a disciplined household, darling. Do you understand what I mean? Students lodge with me, young men, just like you are, I mean just like you will become soon. They are older than you. Boys are apt to become unruly. I say to them all the same thing I say to you: keep yourself clean. Always clean. It is your duty to keep your room tidy. You shall want for nothing. But there are rules in this house. For example, the toilet: I don't want to see any puddles. I know you young men, with your carelessness. Puddles on the floor beside the toilet, that I don't want to see. You are perfectly capable of doing your business in the right place. Do you know what I am talking about? He had bowed his head, a motherless boy in a strange country. And you shall be going to a new school soon, the Academy. Not everybody gets that kind of chance. You are a very unfortunate but also a very lucky boy. Won't that be exciting? Yes, Auntie May, he had said humbly. She had continued: You will be protected here. I will do my best to keep the promises I have made to your dear mother and father. But you are alone now, too much alone. You need to be with boys of your own age now. My student lodgers are too old for you, they have their own lives. It will be good for you to be with boys of your own age. Yes, Auntie May, was all he had been able to repeat, awed by her sternness. But now, as she suddenly embraced him in the room with the piano and with the loudly ticking clock as a background she had abruptly changed her tune, her voice now quavered: Poor, poor boy, she murmured again, more than once. So he was confused and disturbed. He had a strong whiff of her rosy perfume. He could even sense her heart thudding slowly against his squashed ear. It seemed that some considerable time went by while he was imprisoned in this sudden hug, but he endured it with good grace. And at last she released him, and he was able to speak.

Auntie May?

Yes, my child?

So it's OK to read the books?

Yes, of course you can read them.

Auntie May, can I ask another question?

Ask away, my child.

Do you play that piano?

No, I do not.

Who does, then?

The piano was once played by your Uncle. He used to play it every day, before he sickened and took to his bed. (Her eyes flickered heavenwards, indicating the direction in which he could be found.) Nobody has played it since.

I can play the piano, Auntie May.

Can you, really? Ah! Now I remember, something your mother once told me. He's got the gift, she said. Those were her words. I had forgotten. Oh, you poor boy! Would you like to?

I'd like to have a go.

You may play the piano, then, if you wish, but only at certain times of day, and only very quietly, in order not to disturb the neighbours, or my student lodgers, who must have peace to study their books, and above all, not to upset your Uncle in his sick bed. For there is a chance it may redouble his sickness to hear it. Is that quite clear?

Yes, Auntie May.

But Auntie May was no longer there.

The Academy. He had been promised he would go there: it would "provide for his educational and spiritual needs". His aunt had been granted a scholarship, his refugee status and his aunt's staunch faith being considerable assets to the application. She'd shown him a list the school had helpfully provided of the items he would need to take: a grey regulation school jacket; two pairs of grey regulation school trousers; a black Marlborough jacket for Sundays, with pin-stripe trousers; six white shirts; a school tie; a black tie to go with the Marlborough jacket; a pair of black shoes; a grey pullover or jumper; a waterproof coat; a rugby shirt in the school colours; a pair of rugby shorts, white; two pairs of rugby socks, school colours; a pair of rugby boots; a pair of plimsolls; two pairs of pyjamas and a pair of slippers; under-wear and socks (black); a rug; a face flannel. Auntie May would take him on a shopping expedition within the next few days to buy all these things. (What do they mean by a rug? Auntie May wanted to know. Does that mean a small carpet?

Or a kind of blanket? Oh, it's quite exasperating! she exclaimed.) She busied herself with house business, humming a tune the while under her breath. He turned to the piano, sat down. He could pick out a tune quite easily. Anything he heard, he soon found the home note, soon worked it out. He was careful not to play too loudly. Weeks went by. He read many books. He was imprisoned on a desert island, he killed and ate goats, one day he saw footprints in the sand. He was washed up on the shore of an island of little people who overcame him as he slept and tried to pin him down. He re-read some of the books, with increased pleasure and understanding. Summer was no longer the season. The time came. All too soon it came. And he found himself in the town nearest to the promised Academy. Auntie May bought him an ice-cream from the van parked just outside the imperial gardens by the town hall, where multicoloured ducks strutted and pigeons bobbed. Domesticated water lay lapping peacefully beyond, and the ducks swam there. Auntie May and he had come down on the train from London – Uncle had been too unwell to travel. These were the last days of the summer holidays. Later – many years later – he would find bleached photographs, some of which must have been taken by a third party, perhaps begged as a favour from a passer-by, as they were both in them, he and Auntie May; and he would wonder who really was that strange, dark boy, ice-cream in hand with a shock of dark brown ice-cream hair, in a new grey suit and school tie, standing uncomfortably in front of the municipal floral clock, a protagonist in a drama whose details were long gone and are only now being imperfectly reconstructed. It was a last image of freedom, of a sort. But a moment that didn't last. Is that the time? – we must get the bus and find the school, Auntie May exclaimed. The bus was caught at the town's bus station, Auntie May holding the big suitcase, he with the smaller one. The Academy, they were assured by the conductor, was not far up the hill. I will let you know when we get there, he told Auntie May; and, addressing the boy: First day, eh? The boy nodded solemnly. The bus stop was on a hill right by the main gates of the school. Under scudding clouds, vegetation overtumbled the grey stone walls on either side of the open gates, and beyond, at the end of a short drive, loomed the Mansion. They entered the gateway. Auntie May stopped still for a moment, entranced. Look at that, she murmured, nudging her nephew, built in the eighteenth century! So grand! This, she exclaimed approvingly, must be a wonderful place, and promised to be a great opportunity for a boy such as he. If only his dear parents could see him now. If only (a solemn pause) his dear Uncle likewise, who was not with them but would be thinking of him right now. She was sure he would enjoy it here, and he would be well cared for by the Brothers. Other boys and their families were dismounting from large shiny cars and carrying luggage into the porticoed entrance. Tea was being served in the Mansion for the new boys, announced a man in a long black robe who suddenly appeared. The boy, still at his aunt's side, knew that this was one of the Brothers and that the black vestment was called a *soutane*. And the legend had it that in the pocket of this vestment each Brother kept a stout black leather strap intended for chastisement. Another Brother in a black soutane, stocky in build, with glittery spectacles, now approached Auntie May and greeted her by name, with a query signalled at the end of his greeting. She responded happily, and introduced her charge. He shook her hand, and then the boy's. Well, so this is the, ah, scholarship boy himself? said the man with an icy smile. This, Auntie May told the boy, was the chief of the Brothers and the Headmaster of the Academy. I am very hopeful, Auntie May told the Headmaster, that his educational and spiritual needs will be especially well met here in this wonderful place. All the boys' spiritual needs are indeed my, ah, chief concern, intoned the Headmaster. His name was Brother Maguire. Close up, he smelt of pipe tobacco. Welcome to our community, welcome to the school. Please come this way. So beautiful, the facade of the Mansion, Auntie May twittered prettily at Brother Maguire. Ah, he said, wait till you see the view from the back, down the valley and across over the town. The Palladian Folly in our grounds is a famous piece of eighteenth-century architecture. And our Chapel is worth a visit, a fine example of Victorian Gothic. So they chattered. They were led in through the front entrance of the Mansion and up two gloomy flights of massive stone stairs with polished wooden banisters, Brother Maguire now carrying the big suitcase, which he had politely offered to relieve Auntie May of, the boy the smaller one. And our protagonist wondered as he climbed about the leather strap that would be nestling in the pocket of that black soutane ahead. Then along a long corridor whose floorboards were bare, and finally into a dormitory, like a great factory, with light coming in from high windows, where ranks of steel beds lined each wall – an extra double row of them dividing the room down the middle. Here the boy was shown his bed: the second along the left-hand wall. Dust hung in the light that streamed in through the windows. A fair-haired boy, with a self-confident air, who had been sitting on the bed next to his designated one, stood up at the approach of the little party. Ah, this is Schultz-Rayburn – he is also starting as a new boy in the third year this term, said Brother Maguire. Schultz-Rayburn said: How do you do? Hello, said the orphan boy politely. How are you getting on, Schultz-Rayburn? asked the Headmaster. Very well, sir, said the fair-haired boy with alacrity. But the conversation died then. Our protagonist was shown a small wooden bedside cupboard for his personal belongings; there would be a larger closet at the end of the room to store his clothes and other things. And so having deposited his suitcases on his bed for now, they all – the Headmaster, Auntie May and the boy – trooped downstairs again to the Mansion dining hall, where, amid the hubbub of conversation – boys, their parents, the Brothers, and others he was told were "lay teachers" – Auntie May had a cup of tea and the boy had a glass of orange squash and some biscuits. Auntie May tried to make jovial conversation with some of the other parents and guardians. The time went by swiftly, but it was probably about an hour. Her cheek was damp as she hugged the boy and kissed him twice. Your dear mother and father – wouldn't they have been so proud to see you? I know they would. Write me soon, she sternly urged him. And again, outside the Mansion portico in the early evening, before saying the final goodbye: Be sure to write to me and your dear Uncle every week, darling. Don't forget, now. But she is fading ... she is gone, again. She does not re-enter this narrative, we are going somewhere else.

All we recall now is a yellow full moon hanging low over the sea, and the black mass of the sea flecked with a little silver just below it. Is this an image of consciousness? False. We are asleep, and we hear a human voice in the middle of sleep. Are you still in there, darling? You're late up this morning. It is the voice of Sharonne. We emerge from the tent into brightness. Oh, and you're not even dressed properly this morning, you naughty man. We tried to explain: we had been visited again by Sister Dream, but of what we were dreaming we know not any longer. Things that may have happened in the long ago past, or may not. Here's the flask, then, darling, here's your coffee. You got the old one? give it me then. If you had your mobile working I could've give you a wakeup call, ha ha. No, I'm joking, you're better off without it, darling, believe me. I just got alerted, and do you know what it was, all it was was Laverne, a friend of mine, you remember her, look, "changed her profile picture". Earth-shattering, or what?

The cracked windows, the vaulting and the thronging. The great iron radiators placed at intervals, cold now. The smell of pipe tobacco on Brother Maguire's breath. The sound of a distant radio. The clattering and the footsteps advancing and retreating on bare floorboards. These made the greatest impression. The last piece of advice Schulz-Rayburn had given him shortly before lights out was: just watch your step, everybody has to watch their step, that's how it works. And it will all be fine. Schulz-Rayburn – he had spelt his name out – had been at pains to be helpful. He'd been at boarding school before – another school, it was not clear why that had not worked out – so he knew the ropes. His parents were in Nigeria, but he was by no means a black boy. Quite the opposite, in fact. There was a war going on there, so the boy was given to understand. It was unsafe to be there. When the boy awoke, the sun had been shining. The huge dormitory was by no means full, as few of the other boys had yet arrived before the first day of term proper. They were dotted around the room, in their respective beds. They were waking up one by one, and greeting each other. He would have three, maybe five years ahead of him at the Academy. He tried to remember everything Auntie May had said. A bell had rung. In his dressing-gown, he'd followed the others as they trooped, one by one, under the supervision of another Brother in his black soutane, whose name apparently was Brother Callaghan, the House Master, who was accompanied by a large collie bitch everywhere he went, to the communal washroom where he washed his face and brushed his teeth, taking his turn at a row of venerable part-cracked washbasins; then, having dressed in his grey suit and polished black shoes, he followed the others down to breakfast. There were prayers first, led by Brother Maguire. They all had to stand by their places and listen as the Headmaster intoned grace. Schulz-Rayburn, who was next to him, had his eyes fervently closed throughout the prayer, so he closed his too. Finally they were told to take their seats. Schulz-Rayburn already seemed to know what to do; he had already had, he confided, five years of boarding school behind him, including preparatory school, so he was halfway through his trajectory. The refectory – that's what this long room was called – contained a succession of plain wooden tables, with benches on each side to sit on, ranged lengthwise along the narrow part of the building joining the west wing to the Mansion block; it was considerably more dingy than the formal Mansion dining room where the new boys and their parents and guardians had been served tea the day before, but through tall grimy windows he could discern a panoramic view of English parkland. This must be the grounds the Headmaster had mentioned. By now, the sun had gone behind clouds. It was a mysterious and enticing vista of a sort he had never encountered, blurring into soft, distant edges beyond which nothing could be seen. But here in the refectory Irish girls in uniform with sour faces now emerged and dumped metal trays of dry toast on each table in turn, each precious round to be grabbed and plastered with margarine. Then other metal trays arrived with flabby fragments of bacon and toughened roundels of fried egg swimming in a shallow sea of grease; and there were also metal urns for tea and coffee. He waited his turn politely. A few of the boys turned to look at him; some seemed puzzled or vexed, one or two smiled and introduced themselves, or briefly explained the protocols to be followed, but the majority paid no attention to him at all while they renewed or made acquaintances elsewhere. Schulz-Rayburn nudged him again and said helpfully and knowledgeably: The first week will be hell, but it'll be all right after that. After the boys had all finished breakfast, they had to stand to attention again collectively by the refectory tables until officially dismissed, this time by Brother Callaghan, whose dog had accompanied him into the refectory; then they filed out and were free to do what they liked. Lessons would not begin until the following day, by which time the whole school would have assembled. He exhaled with relief that it wasn't after all too bad. Another boy showed him the library in the Mansion block, which had wood panelling on the walls and the day's broadsheet newspapers laid out on a series of lecterns. That was impressive. He remembered he had left the little notebook and pen he always carried everywhere back in the dormitory. So he made his way back through the refectory again (where all the breakfast things had been tidied away by the staff) towards the dormitory in the Mansion block. In an alcove off that spinal corridor – he hadn't quite got the topography of the building internalised yet – he came upon an old piano; you would think it the twin of the one in Auntie May's drawing room. A piano! Nobody was around, so with apprehension (lest it be forbidden) he sat on the stool and lifted the lid. A silent echo. He seemed to be positioned well below the keyboard, but he remembered that it was possible to fiddle with the piano stool at Auntie May's to adjust the height, and so it proved with this one. Now the keys were at a nice distance. He placed his hands on them. The first chord he essayed with his left hand frightened him by reverberating sonorously throughout, so it seemed, the entire building. But nobody arrived to forbid such sounds. So when the reverberations had died down he tried again, at first sinking his fingers into the keys at random, then after a while attempting the few tunes he remembered, which the instrument seemed unused to, you would say, but warmed to eventually – and in this fashion it seemed an hour or two went by. Nobody came by or troubled him. Until a bell rang. He looked round. A black shadow loomed, and he caught his breath: it was Brother Callaghan, the House Master (with the dog in attendance) (the smell of the dog), who had called his name. He got up. The Brother nodded and said: That was very nice. But that bell is to announce lunch.

Our protagonist discovered that lunchtime was very much the same procedure as for breakfast, except that you were supposed to serve yourself from the salad tray. The food did not have any colour, or taste of anything much. The other boys mostly talked over him. In the afternoon, once it was finished, he thought he would explore that park he could see through the windows, if he could reach it. He particularly wanted to see the valley, and the Palladian Folly, whatever that was, that had been mentioned by Brother Maguire. He couldn't find a doorway directly opening onto it, but eventually saw that by going out the front door through which he had been delivered the day before he could follow a path round the extremity of the building and come upon it that way. By that time it had really clouded over and started to drizzle in an extremely fine, tepid, misty fashion. He heard some shouting. On the lawn at the back of the school thus

revealed, a bunch of the boys he recognised from the refectory as being of his year group, in shorts and sundry rugby
and T-shirts, were having an impromptu game of football –
four little piles of coats serving as goalposts. He stood and
watched. The ball rolled towards him and he kicked at it
tentatively so that it dribbled back to the boy with the red
face who was coming to retrieve it. The boy looked at him
with curiosity. Over on the other side of the lawn an argument had begun to develop between a few of the others over
a ruling which could not be definitively settled in the
absence of a referee. While this was going on, the boy
addressed him:

Are you the scholarship boy?

He was confused.

Are you the scholarship boy? the red-faced boy persisted. After the initial shock of the confrontation, he
appeared friendly enough, though you never could tell.

Yes, he said. It seemed the easiest of the possible answers.

You can play with us, if you like. We're one short. Do you
have plimsolls?

Plimsolls?

Yes. Don't you know what plimsolls are?

A pair of plimsolls. That had been on the list of things
Auntie May had had to buy. They were sports shoes, it
turned out. Yes, I do, he said.

Go to your dorm and fetch them, commanded the boy.

He did, and, quickly divesting himself of his uniform,
put on a pair of shorts and the rugby shirt Auntie May had
packed. Thus clad, he returned, joined the game and spent
most of the afternoon playing football on the lawn; or at
least, running around vigorously and enjoyably if to very
little effect.

You're not very good, are you? said the red-faced boy,
whose name was Teddy – though he probably meant no

harm. An advantage gained was that he was starting to get to know the other boys' names, or nicknames, as they shouted to each other: In the middle, Teddy! Great goal, Charlie! You spastic, Butters! Spastic was the insult most commonly hurled. He didn't know what it meant. The light was beginning to fade by the time the game came to an end, by apparent mutual consent. One by one the boys wandered off, so he started to make his way back to the dorm. But he was distracted on the way by noises and voices, other boys congregating, boys he had not yet seen. The school was starting to fill up. He discovered, in a large gloomy room off a corridor, a television set, the biggest he had ever seen, on a rostrum in front of several rows of seats with leaking upholstery. A boy was trying to tune it to a channel, while another desultory group stood by – but only an indistinct grey image could be obtained. The other boys shouted advice. The picture cleared. More boys arrived and sat down on the shabby seats. This was the final evening before lessons were due to start. He sat down. There was a last leisure hour before supper. More boys had come into the television room, some arguing and jeering at the screen. The programme was *Top of the Pops*. After a short while the our protagonist got up and wandered back into the corridor towards the Mansion and then into the wood-panelled library. It was quiet there; only one other, much older boy slumped in a leather armchair reading a magazine about cars. This boy did not pay him any heed. It was quiet here. He spent some time standing at the long lectern, turning the enormous flimsy pages of the day's newspapers that were secured there. Great and solemn events were outlined and commented on. He looked for any reports of the war in Nigeria that Schultz-Rayburn had told him about. There was not much, but there was news of hurricanes and floods. Finally, growing tired of his perusing, he decided to go back up to the dormitory, perhaps to read there one of the books he had brought with him, with permission, from Auntie May's. (He had not known what to do with them other than stuff them inside the small bedside cabinet he had been allocated.) But as he made for the door, he found he had to pass the older boy reading his magazine. He made for the gap between the boy's feet and the low table in the middle of the room. As he did so, without seeming to look, the older boy deliberately stretched his legs out and he suddenly found himself tripping over them, falling, grabbing for the edge of the table. Was it an accident, a deliberate provocation or a joke? Uncertainly, without thinking, he called out: Hey, watch it! The older boy looked up at him, said nothing in response as he left the library. But moments later, out in the Mansion hallway, he felt a violent push in the back. The older boy had come out after him. He backed fearfully into one of the massive columns that held up the ceiling here. The older boy's big contorted face was inches from his. He had close-cropped fair hair and the bluest, most piercing eyes he had ever seen. He grabbed the younger boy by the tie.

Do you want your head bashed in?

No, he said – more surprised than afraid.

Well, you're [bad word] well going to if you don't look out, you [bad word] stupid little [bad word he had never heard before].

His face was enormous, granite-like in its composition – like a granite planet was a phrase that popped incongruously into his head – with those blue eyes set in it, set in a gaze of malevolence that was quite astonishing and unprecedented. His voice was deep and rough though his accent was what he had learned was "posh". Then after what seemed to amount to an eternity of face-to-face contact he let go of the tie and was gone.

The boy was badly shaken.

Back in the dorm, the only other person there was red-faced Teddy from the earlier football session who was carefully arranging his possessions on his bedside cabinet. Trying to keep his voice from quavering, he described the incident he had just experienced. Teddy listened, nodded sympathetically. Ah. That would be Grech, he declared gravely after considering all the evidence. He pretty well rules the roost around here.

Is he the Head Boy, then?

No, no, no, said Teddy, they always appoint some nonentity, somebody saintly, as Head Boy. Not Grech. He wouldn't do. But he is Captain of Rugby. He's in the sixth form. He's been in the sixth form for years, I think maybe this is his fourth year. Because he keeps failing his A Levels, so his parents keep sending him back to the school, apparently, ha ha. That's unfortunate for you, coming up against Grech, and you only just arrived. You want to stay out of his way. You don't want to give him cheek. Or any of his cronies.

Cheek?

Yes, cheek. You know what cheek is?

I don't think I gave him cheek, said the boy. There must be some mistake.

Teddy smiled indulgently, as though to indicate there was a lot to learn here.

There would be a light supper in the refectory before bedtime, Brother Callaghan told him. But as he was getting ready to go down he heard his name called. This time it was called in a rather piping, uncertain tone. He looked round, startled. A much younger boy was standing in the doorway of this, the third-form dorm, evidently nervous of entering a place that would have been strictly out of bounds to him and the rest of his year group. This young lad intoned his name a second time and remained standing in the doorway. That's me, he said, went towards the doorway and waited for a response. Our protagonist and the younger boy stood a yard or two from each other. The younger one said, with a slight stammer: G-grech would like to see you.

Grech would like to see me?

Yes.

Well, I was just going down to the refectory for supper. I can talk to him there.

No, said the smaller boy, he wants to see you now. I'm to take you to his room. He stood there in the doorway, unwilling to enter the sacred space. His school uniform grey suit fitted him badly, his face was thin, he had smeary glasses on his snub little nose. And he blinked nervously.

Now?

Yes. I'm to take you.

This was new and shocking. Looking on the bright side, maybe Grech wanted to apologise to him personally for his actions? Or maybe that was too much to hope for. But if not, if Grech still felt animosity, this might nevertheless be a chance to clear the air, to explain to him that he had not meant any harm, that when he had said "watch it" to him, Grech, in the library after he, Grech, stretched his legs and caused him to trip over them he was only jesting, or bantering. He had not meant anything by it, it was all a misunderstanding. He had noticed that jesting and bantering formed the chief mode of communication among many of the boys here at the Academy. Surely Grech would see that, therefore, and would himself then apologise? There would be a clearing up of this misunderstanding, a shaking of hands at least, even if they could not go so far as to agree to be friends. So he said to the smaller boy, Well, you'd better take me to him, I expect. And the smaller boy, clearly relieved that he was going to come quietly, and therefore to absolve him of any responsibility, seemed to cheer up a bit and immediately mumbled: Follow me!

So he did. He followed the youngster out of the dorm and into the passage outside. And he thought the boy ahead of him was going to turn right as usual and begin to descend the marble staircase with the polished wooden banisters, down to the Mansion's ground floor, but instead he continued along the corridor which was quite dark, and then he seemed to suddenly disappear; but he hadn't, he had turned left into the opening of another staircase, a much narrower one, leading upwards. And the small boy was waiting inside the opening for him to arrive before continuing. He asked the youngster: What's your name, by the way? Boyce, he replied. Boyce? Pleased to meet you, Boyce. My name is– but the boy interrupted, We know your name. Of course you do, he said. Follow me, said Boyce, who seemed much more confident now, and began to climb the stairs. The lighting was rather dim. It was really just security lighting. One flight was negotiated, they came to a half-landing, then another flight, then another. It seemed to him that Boyce was leading him up the inside of a tower, a lighthouse; there seemed no limit to the height they would reach. But at last they reached a top landing. There was light coming through onto it from a dirty window. And Boyce led him into a long straight corridor, bare floorboards, with doors in the walls on either side, another window ahead. He stopped at the last door on the right before the window and knocked on it. The door opened. It was not Grech. It was another senior boy, thin and tall, with sandy hair and a thin wide mouth; he was in the regulation school grey jacket and trousers, but instead of a white shirt and the school tie he wore a multi-coloured Hawaiian shirt under it. He barked: Did you bring him, Boyce? Then he immediately saw our protagonist, and beckoned him briskly into the room, making space for him to enter. To the young boy, he said: Wait outside, Boyce.

What our protagonist saw when he entered was this. A pleasant bedroom, carpeted (unlike any of the other rooms he had so far seen in the Academy) and with curtains drawn back at a window that let in the last of the dusky September light. Though the bare bulb in the centre of the ceiling was already lit. There was a wooden wardrobe, a desk and chair. Covering the walls were coloured photographic images, mostly centrefolds ripped out of what our protagonist, even in his innocence, realised were girlie magazines and tacked up with sellotape: young women in no or next to no clothes, inviting his pubescent gaze. On the ceiling over the bed, illuminated by the lightbulb, sprawled ecstatically the woman he recognised as Marilyn Monroe, naked against a blood-red background – an image that many years later, many years after these events had faded from the memory of most of the participants, might have been termed *iconic* – but that overused term was not in currency at this time. Returning to the actual occupants of the room: seated in an armchair next to the window was another senior boy, so senior that he had advanced stubble on his chin, almost a beard. He was in the school jacket and trousers, but with an open-necked white shirt, and his feet were bare. Standing in the opposite corner of the room, unnoticed till he turned his head, was a third boy, clad in an oriental silk dressing-gown patterned in green and gold flames and dragons, and slippers. And lying on the bed that formed the centrepiece of the room, his head and shoulders propped up on cushions, in rugby shirt and shorts, his powerfully muscled legs bare, was, recognisably, Grech.

Our protagonist thought it prudent to come straight to the point with a conciliatory word, an apology even.

I'd just like to – he began, but got no further.

Yeah, this is the [bad name], said Grech nodding lacon- ically to the friend who had ushered him in and had shut the door in Boyce's face. That's him, all right, Smythe.

At this, Smythe advanced rapidly up to him and pushed his chest smartly, so that he fell against a chair and found himself suddenly sitting down.

Get up, snarled Smythe. He stood up, his legs trembling. And Smythe added in a matter-of-fact way: We don't like [bad word] [bad word]s who don't know their place here.

I didn't mean –

Grech said in an instant, laughing, It's not your place to mean.

The three other boys in the room echoed gloating, appre- ciative laughs that rippled softly in the dim light. And by the way the library, added Smythe, is out of bounds to little third-form pricks like you. Did you know that?

No.

I think he knows it now, murmured the boy in the dress- ing gown from his corner.

Smythe again: You keep your head down. Or you get it smashed. You hear?

I'll keep my head down, don't worry.

Listen, [Badword]face, we're not worrying, believe me, said Smythe.

More laughter.

My name's not –

We know your name.

They knew his name. How was this possible? He was a new boy. He had only just been enrolled in the school. He himself knew hardly any of the other boys' names yet, apart from Schulz-Rayburn, Teddy ... who else? little Boyce, who would be outside in the corridor right now, and of course Smythe, who had admitted him to this sanctum. And Grech.

How do you know my name? he asked in wonder.

How do we know your name, well, well, said Grech from his bed, blowing nonchalantly on his fingers, Maggot keeps us all informed.

Maggot?

Brother Maguire, the Headmaster to you. He's in our pocket, isn't he, lads?

There was a universal murmur of assent, and hilarity at the thought of Maggot in their pocket.

So, continued Grech evenly, don't even think of bleating to Maggot about anything you don't like, because it all comes right back here. You understand?

There was a knock on the door. Grech said to Smythe: If that's Boyce, tell him to [bad word]ing wait. Smythe opened the door. It was not Boyce, it was a girl. Our protagonist instantly recognised one of the Irish girls who had served meals in the refectory, but she was out of her nylon servant's uniform now and wearing a mini-skirt, her eyes heavily shadowed. It's Colleen, said Smythe, turning to Grech. Tell her not now, replied Grech, tell her to come back later. Can you come back later, Colleen? said Smythe. The girl nodded, casting a nervous glance at our protagonist, and he shut the door.

Our protagonist stared fixedly in front of him during all this. He was trying to understand. Through the window he saw the evening continued to darken.

You like the view from here? said Grech, noticing his gaze. Then, speaking to the boy at the window: Show him the view!

The stubbled, barefoot boy at the window rose from his seat and flung the heavy sash up, while simultaneously Smythe pushed him roughly in the back so that he stumbled towards the window. And the stubbled boy caught him and thrust him over the sill. And suddenly he was hanging over, he thought

he was going to fall out of the window, the boy had grasped
him in his big fist by the back of the neck and held him there.
A cool blast of air had hit him. The view was of the valley at
the back of the school, far far below, the light fading to the
west, over the treeline, very picturesque as Auntie May might
have commented, and he heard Grech's voice, sneering, It's a
long way down, isn't it? He could see the valley sloping away,
very green, and a glint of water in the middle of it, with an
ancient and elaborate columnated stone building bridging the
water – that must be the famous Palladian Folly – and woodland on either side, but it was all very very far off though seem-
ing to pulse to get further away and come nearer by turns as
though he were being alternately dropped and retrieved
by the scruff of his neck and Grech's sneering voice
    acting as punctuation the while and then everything
        went blue but it wasn't the sky it was blue light
            flooding consciousness coming out of nowhere
                and everywhere and everything was vibrating
            the blue material above and all around
        with its distinctive odour. They let him go then
        there wasn't much more of it he was
            pulled back from the edge he heard
                Smythe opening the door and calling out
                    Boyce! you little turd! and had the
                        impression that Boyce had been
                            sitting on the floor against the wall
                                outside in the corridor had shot
                            upright at the sound of the call
                        and had resumed his duties
                    escorting him down all the way
                down all the staircases until
            finally he was back in his
            own dorm where
        Schulz-Rayburn returning
    from his supper found him

lying on his bed weeping the
  enormous embarrassment
      of this so that Schulz-Rayburn
          didn't know what to do
                      or say it appeared
                      the other new boy was
                              crying best to say
                              nothing maintaining a
                                  dignified silence would
                                  help to ease the
                              embarrassment
                          while the other
                  new boy was
              mumbling
          my name
    he was
  saying they
  knew my
      name

7 the film crew

So far, so far. When you are on a trail. As if that could lead to everything. As if anything could be everything. As if nothing could be everything. As if everything could be everything. Or everything nothing. What are we trying to say? When you are on a trail that promises to lead to marvellous secrets being revealed (at last!) and then suddenly you realise you are just following your old footprints all over again, that you have been circling, not breaking new ground, not at all, the trail coming back to the same old thing, the scent recently discovered merely your old scent after all, well, it's discouraging. It is and it isn't. It is and it is. It isn't, is it? Well, it may be. Something may be there anyway. Or there may be something in it. Something is there, we know it, or we seem to know it and act as if we did. Surely there's something in that? That is what we are trying to say. If we act as if we know it, then maybe we do know it. A forlorn hope, maybe, but still. All we have is what we think we know. It is of our kind and the only kind we know. *Ipso facto* and *sui generis*. Ah, let's get back, let's get back down in the groove, as the jazzers used to say. The tide coming in and the tide going out, in that rhythm, in counterpoint to the rhythm of the days. That's a different one. So we begin again. Always in the rhythm. That rhythm, or the other one, the contrapuntal movement of the two rhythms. The rhythm of the tide and the rhythm of the days. And always begin again. What was there? What remains in memory? There was a yellow full moon hanging low over the sea, and the black mass of the sea flecked with a little silver just below it. Just a little, at the horizon, the rest of it huge black. That's it! Just before dawn, maybe. And we are asleep, and we hear a human voice in the middle of sleep, in the middle of everything, a voice we did not wish to hear. That voice calling our name. Calling our name, imagine that! Are you in the fucking *zoo*? *Are you in the fucking zoo?* Everything was vibrating. We have been down that rabbit hole where everything went deep blue; we have been there and done that. Begin from there, then – or, to put it another way, from here. Where? *Here.* So here we are in our quarters on the beach, thinking and observing, observing and thinking. But *are* we in our quarters? In our station? What is that blue material? Everything is vibrating. Everything is calm. Everything that can be observed will be observed. If it's observed, it's happening, or has happened. We can say this happened, and that happened. Things happen, and maybe happen again, before they cease to happen. So far, so far. Then we can move on. Because we have a shape, we have identified a shape, we can move on. This shape moves into that, and that into the other, and collectively we are approaching a new shape of shapes, which will be a consolidation of all the shapes that have occurred; you have to keep moving in order to arrive at this consolidation where it all comes to a standstill, but of course it never arrives, the standstill that is, and that's the whole point, it never stands still. Because that shape of all the shapes itself becomes an element to be taken into what subsumes it. And so it never ends. Morning has come. And the shapes constantly shift. We are prompted to these thoughts especially by the observation, with interest and curiosity, of the movements of those few figures who have taken to assembling on a certain day every week, early in the day, indeed as early as sunup, in these long days of summer, a little way off from our quarters towards the east, in the place where the beach is interrupted by a floor of concrete. It's probable that this concrete floor is all that remains of a previous demolition, the only evidence of a building that once stood here. But it has now been repurposed by this group of people. They meet on a Friday morning, here on the beach. The day of the week was noted the first time it came to our attention, and now the activity acts as a date marker, conveying the information that today is Friday. Sometimes there are as few as four individuals including the leader, but more often six, seven, even eight. Never more than eight. Almost certainly never more than eight. They are more or less the same people week after week, though from time to time different ones appear, and may remain the following week and establish themselves in the group, or may not. Sometimes a regular is not present, and may or may not reappear thereafter. But, identifiably, this is a group. After they arrive, after a short time, they stand apart from each other, already with a certain measure of stillness to start off with. It is a martial art they are attempting, under guidance, most likely Tai Chi, on that floor of concrete. They are mostly in the later stages of their lives. Their obvious leader and mentor, always present, is a woman of some stature, not Chinese, younger than all of them, slim and with a bronzed body and a head of plentiful dark hair, often caught in a bandanna. The group have their attention directed towards her, but through her to the slow movements they are themselves making in the early morning. They slink serpentinely through all the movements indicated to them by her, their mentor and guide. As they move and make their shapes, they are always approaching stillness, but never attain it finally; what seems like the final shape they arrive at and hold at any one instance is never final, always provisional. So far, so far. And that would seem to be the point, and it's accepted by the group, but eventually after half an hour or so (it's hard to estimate the clock time without a functioning wristwatch or device), by common consensus it would seem, or because of something that has been said that we can't catch from here, they leave their last shapes hanging in the morning air – that, then, really being the final one – then return abruptly to their normal movements, which are quicker and less stylised; picking up their belongings from the ground where they have placed them, for example, or speaking again cheerfully to their mentor and to each other, then beginning to drift off, some in ones and twos, others remaining within the main group as it drifts. And always it's as if nothing has happened, but something did. Or the reverse. As if, but also and so. Something happened, but whether it was real or imaginary it isn't possible to say. Notes have been taken by us, but only belatedly and not very assiduously: suffice it to say that the group (excluding the leader) to the best of our knowledge never numbered more than eight or less than four, though the exact number on each occasion has not been recorded with sufficient rigour; that it assembled weekly at what might be judged around seven or eight in the morning and dispersed around half an hour later; that the assembly and its activities started manifesting around the spring or early summer, and continued on a weekly basis, but have more recently ceased so far as can be ascertained, for this group of people have not reappeared for three weeks now (at the time of recording this) and may therefore be supposed to have suspended operations due to the coming of autumn, or for some other reason. So each week subsequently when it was estimated Friday had arrived the area was observed, but the group did not reappear. A few mornings ago there had been some hopes of a resumption, with the appearance of a group of three approaching figures, trudging along the beach from the east at around that time of the morning – and it was almost certainly a Friday – but as this group neared our quarters, it was quickly resolved into three men in dark blue jumpsuits with yellow hi-vis piping carrying yellow and blue helmets, on the trail of something – their own trail or quest. This was something different. They were the coastguards; admittedly they had been observed before, but from afar, not this close. Their boots crunched on the shingle. They chatted and bantered among themselves. These were very different shapes they were making in the early morning air. And one of them now peeled off in a gentle arc, making for and gradually approaching our station. This caused apprehension at first. He revealed himself to be a big, eager man with most of his life before him. His dark hair was rumpled, he cradled his helmet in his right arm. He called out to us as he came nearer. Excuse me, mate – and we acknowledged the greeting with a nod, we appreciated the respect – excuse me mate, but you wouldn't happen to have seen a small vessel offshore here? This morning? Yeah, early hours of this morning. What sort of small vessel? What are you looking for? We're investigating an incident, he said. An incident, that's all he would say. No, was our answer, no small vessel had been observed, and with this a machine roar swiftly swelled in the sky, drowning our voices for a few seconds, and a dark shape loomed overhead: the Coastguard Service helicopter, which has been observed on occasion before, but, again, not at such close quarters, its rotors whirring as it passed and receded, making its way back slowly over the sea in a south-westerly direction. Cheers, mate, the young man, on whose face could now be seen tiny beads of sweat, said by way of valediction, as soon as he could be heard above the ebbing noise of the helicopter, his left arm raised in acknowledgement, and then shouting at his colleagues as he turned and made his way back over to them: No, he ain't seen nothing! He was no longer talking to us now. Are you looking for refugees? we asked of his departing form, are you looking for refugees? but he paid no attention, for our role in the proceedings had ceased and we were clearly of no further use to the operation.

But maybe twenty minutes later the van arrived. It was natural to associate one event with the other. The refugees and the van. So it was that morning, a morning like any other, except inasmuch as nothing is like anything else.

Because we had been dreaming of the refugees recently. Sister Dream presented this offering of hers to us on several occasions, in various guises. It was natural that this should be so, because refugees had been in the news recently – not that we currently have any handy means of monitoring the news regularly, but so we had gathered from broadcasts and programmes on the screen in the Shell Beach Project TV room, for instance, or from newspapers discarded by holiday-makers from time to time. There had been increasing reports of refugees being sighted off the coast, packed precariously into small inflatable boats, coming from we know not where heading to they knew not where. They and we, but are we here in our tent, is that the dark blue stuff we perceive in the dream? Or are we adrift, hopelessly, being carried across the immense channel with little hope of arriving at an imagined destination? In our troubled sleep it seemed to us that we were no longer alone in the tent but that people were starting to enter, at first one or two but then more and more of them, familiar faces many of them, until it seemed as though everybody we had ever known was beginning to pack into the confined space, which was becoming intolerable, the smell of the indigo canvas now mingling with the various odours of perspiration from bodies vying for room and fighting for air. One by one, they joined the company here until finally there was no more room. And the floor began slowly to heave up and down in great rolling waves, without cease, so that stomachs too began to heave and acid tastes began to form in our throats. But where were we anyway? Nobody could remember the beginning of the voyage and nobody knew where the endpoint might be or when it might be reached. And although it had seemed at first that the crowd packed in here consisted of everybody we had ever known, the suspicion grew gradually that this was not in fact so, that those people jammed into our face were after all strangers, we had never seen any of them before, old people, young men, mothers with desperate, bawling infants, sick people, the whole caboodle of humankind. We had identified with the refugees, we desperately wanted to identify with the refugees, they were a point of reference, a last hope. But their faces, jammed close to our face, were no longer known to us, as we had at first thought, but were becoming maps of strange and uncharted territories. Deeply familiar, yet deeply inscrutable. Each face had a history behind it, there was no doubt of that, but a history that could not be told, that would never be told. There was a gulf and we were engulfed. The dream seemed endless, but like everything else it eventually did come to an end. Night itself was coming to end, and morning would dissolve everything. But then waking from this horror, it all took an age to process, to separate the dream objects from the facts, to line up the dream objects one by one and tick them off as illusions even as the hours before dawn were spent. So that was natural, to make true or false associations in the early light, in the tent-boat or outside the tent-boat in the chill, on the shingle that was no longer heaving, that had thankfully become static, though even so we felt the urgent need to unzip the closure and step out onto the cold shingle and the open air of early morning for relief. But enough: this is a lengthy way of preambling that that was the morning the coastguards and then subsequently the van arrived. It had appeared at first sight to belong to a news crew, and we jumped to the conclusion, naturally enough, that the television news was following the story, if there was a story, about the boat refugees, if indeed there were any. But the only information that had actually been imparted by the young man in the coastguard uniform was that an "incident" had occurred, an incident perhaps involving a small vessel, so there was a lot of extrapolation needed there. Incidents occur all the time, they are observed daily round here on the foreshore, hourly, even minute by minute. No minute goes by without there being an incident that is capable of being reported, if there is anybody interested, which most of the time there is not. For example, a squabble between two of the herring gulls over ownership of the head of a mackerel. Incidents are of themselves trivial, in that sense, unless attention is unduly drawn to them, in which case they become non-trivial. But is it the interest, in itself, that magnifies the incident into one that could be described as non-trivial, or is there a quality in the incident, of itself, regardless of whether it actually causes interest, that makes it significant, that makes it worth reporting – worth drumming up some interest in? Or is it the conjunction of the incident with the occurrence of some other incident? If another incident follows rapidly upon the first, that is. Well, in this case, that morning on the foreshore, there was indeed a second incident, after the coastguards, and that was the arrival of the van. The surmise that the two incidents were linked – incident multiplied by incident makes non-trivial incident – led to speculation on our part, awakened our interest. As if nothing could be anything. As if anything could be anything. The van, which had a logo on its side and the name OSIRISIS PRODUCTIONS displayed prominently, was observed from afar. It was observed to arrive perhaps twenty minutes perhaps half an hour after the coastguards had disappeared; it parked at the edge of the beach, close to where the men had erected temporary fencing around the derelict beach huts, preparatory to demolishing them; people were observed to get out, we counted them, there were five in all, so far as we could make out, young people it seemed – very young, some of them – laughing and joking, two of them wielding film or video cameras on tripods, while another fetched other pieces of equipment from the back of the van, equipment that appeared to consist of assemblages of electronic gear – microphones on poles, rolls of cable, lights, black boxes, silvery metal packing cases. All of this, in conjunction with the timing of their appearance so shortly after the intervention of the coastguards, is why we had supposed them to be a news crew. It turned out, as we shall see later, to be an inaccurate supposition, but it had some validity. For the refugees had been in the news, as has been explained. But we are forgetting. Let the focus return to OSIRISIS PRODUCTIONS. The five young people who had spilled out of the van began to set up their operations next to the temporarily fenced-off beach huts, to the left of our station (as one looks towards the sea), and started scoping the terrain and practising for whatever it was they had in mind. Two had set up cameras. The leading figures, who seemed to be directing operations and hyperactively issuing instructions, were two slim individuals, almost identical, clad in luminous T-shirts – respectively sour lime-yellow and mauve-pink – that stood out against the grey of the morning. We meanwhile continued to sit on the bench contemplating the ever changing/never changing sea in front of us, while resigning ourself to the inevitability of their eventual approach. And sure enough, before long the group started to move in our direction, the twin luminosities in the lead.

Hi, how you doing? It was the lime-yellow that spoke first. We nodded – an affirmative gesture indicating our acceptance of the world as it is, for better or worse.

We're film-makers, he explained as he came up to us. Please don't mind us. We don't mean to disturb you. I'm Solomon, and this is my sister Salamanda.

We now saw that there were minute differences, aside from the colour of their T-shirts, that distinguished the male from the female in these slender and apparently at first androgynous twin creatures. We nodded again.

Can we do anything for you? asked Solomon in the lime-yellow.

Stand out of my light, we replied. (We couldn't resist that.)

Oh, sorry.

A classical reference, we added by way of explanation, but he appeared not to understand that we were channelling Diogenes when confronted by Alexander the Great. It may have been a stupid and unwise joke on our part. There was a pause.

You here a lot?

All the time, we responded, except for those times we are not.

Listen, I don't suppose you've seen ... well, you probably wouldn't know him. We were expecting to rendezvous here with a musician called Unstable Cliff Edge ...? – the interrogatory upward cadence inviting recognition.

Cliff, we said. Yes, we confirmed that we knew him well, though hadn't seen him for a few days, maybe even a few weeks. It was hard to maintain a calendar here on the beach, we explained.

Wow, you know him! chimed in Salamanda in the mauve-pink. He's a legend! So exciting, she said, our parents used to be fans of Suckling Rats. We grew up listening to them.

Yes, we said that we were aware of the work of the legendary punk era musician and his erstwhile band, though only recently by way of a video on a mobile phone; that he was indeed a local inhabitant, and that we counted him among our friends, though he had so far as we recalled not mentioned that he was going to meet up with film-makers here.

Well, we contacted him a while ago, said Solomon. We want him to star in this feature film we're planning to make. He said he would meet us here today, about half an hour ago.

We said, in confidence, that timekeeping was perhaps not Clifford Edgeworth's best suit.

That figures, said Solomon nonchalantly. So you weren't into punk music back in the day?

We agreed that we were not, and added that, to the contrary, in those days we used to be intimate with the late operatic mezzo-soprano Tabula Rasa, she of the chiselled cheekbones and scented candles. Who had sung at Covent Garden, at the Met, and once at La Scala. We could tell many stories about her, we suggested, should the brother and sister team require more material for their film. She was a woman of some stature, well-proportioned. Her eyes were sparkling and her knees were very tall. Her voice when she was in her pomp was capable of either captivating infants or rattling bay windows, as might be required. She may have been described as a *diva*, whatever that meant; she certainly had the authentic scowl at times of a fashion model or the like. But she declined from that peak. As did the Suckling Rats, frankly, as do we all.

Wow, even better! exclaimed Salamanda. Do you mind if we film you?

Not at all, we assured her.

Great, said Solomon. Let's have some lighting here, it's a little dark this morning, he called to one of his colleagues, a small, pale-faced girl who was wielding a large lamp. What ensued was akin to a new sunrise. A young man in dreadlocks meanwhile set up a camera in front of us. Solomon fussed around while Salamanda moved a big fluffy microphone on a stick closer to our face and the dreadlocked youth focused the camera on us. Great, said Solomon again. Just checking sound levels.... OK, Sal? Right, sir, say something, anything.

We leaned forward and spoke into the microphone: I have no desire to demonstrate, surprise, amuse, or persuade. My goal is absolute rest. To know nothing, to teach nothing, to want nothing, to sense nothing, to sleep, and then to sleep more.

There was a pause.

That's great, said Solomon encouragingly. Is this your philosophy?

No, not at all, we replied. It is a quotation from a poet called Charles Baudelaire.

Wow, cool. Now, just tell us, in your own words, how you came to be living here.

They crowded around us, seriously and intently. It was necessary to say something more. So we provided them with a very abbreviated history of the circumstances that had led us to dwell here. It was a summary, it was sparing of details, you might even say it was bowdlerised to a certain extent, stripped of anything that might have been distressing or controversial or that might have bored the listener. Parts of the narrative were extemporised, in order to improve the story arc. The endpoint of it was that we had been here for a year or more now. That there had been initiatives on the part of certain agencies – statutory, voluntary and commercial, each with their own agenda – to move us on from here, perhaps permanently. That there were challenges entailed in these putative plans, and that personally we had decidedly mixed feelings about such plans. All of this seemed to interest the twin film-makers further.

We paused to allow questions.

I notice you're writing in your notebook quite a lot, while you sit on that bench, said Solomon. Can I ask – just out of interest, I don't wish to be nosy – what it is you're writing?

This, we stated, we are writing *this*. We pointed first to the notebook in our hand and then to our surroundings. We let another pause intervene. But he seemed, judging by the quality of his attention, and the vague smile and slight nodding of his head after we answered him, to want more detail. So we expanded a little: Chiefly, we write words. We have been doing this for a long time – for many years before we even arrived at this beach. In fact, we have been doing this ever since words started to form in our infant mouth. Words are sounds that sleep in our head. Once they emerge, for example by being spoken or written down, they become something else, a fusion between thought (or sense) and sound. That's all there is to it. We might write a sentence one day. Then the next day we might cross it out. So far, so far.

Ah, I see. *Cut!*

This is going to be fantastic, exclaimed Salamanda as she removed the microphone from the vicinity of our face. We haven't got a set script, you see, we're improvising as we go along.

They conferred among themselves, apparently concerning mainly technical matters. While this was going on, we continued to contemplate the sea from our perch on the bench. And finally Solomon turned to us, with a gesture to indicate he had forgotten something important.

By the way, what is your name, if you don't mind me asking?

The question presented us with a challenge. If we were to feature in such a film – though we were not sure we wanted this –we would have to get it right. After some brief thought we replied, Grech.

Grech?

That's right.

Is that a first name or a last name?

(No answer.)

Can you spell it?

G-R-E-C-H.

Salamanda wrote this down in a notebook she had produced. There was more private conferring between the twin film-makers in their sour lime-yellow and mauve-pink T-shirts, luminous in the grey morning.

Listen, Grech, said Solomon, returning with great seriousness, I tell you what. We're going to make the story of your life.

What we want to know, added Salamanda excitedly, is what you're all about, really, *who is the real Grech?*

8 the real Grech

Mr Clifford Edgeworth turned up the following day, bright as ever. He arrived suddenly at our station where we were seated just as OSIRISIS PRODUCTIONS were beginning to set up for the second day's filming. He punched us playfully in the side as a form of greeting. How are you doing, Phil? he shouted in our ear. Where had he been? Where when? Yesterday, we clarified. He had mistaken the date, he said. But no worries, here he was now. Ready to go. Ready to roll. And he made rolling motions with both his stick-like hands. Ready to rock and roll, we suggested, and he liked that. He really liked that. He guffawed. Cliff has an incongruous guffaw, throwing his head back, in the manner of a retired army colonel safe in his club. But he was right in there that morning. That's to say, here. Completely present. For Cliff, there is only the here and now; the future is unimportant, even non-existent. We are always *in media res*, in the middle of the thing or in the middle of nowhere, as one pleases. So then the twins, Solomon and Salamanda, who had been directing the setup in the middle distance ever since the van had disgorged its contents for the second morning, ran over to us when they saw him arrive. It was colder this morning: they were now wearing almost identical dark hoodies, which made them difficult to distinguish from each other. Are you Unstable Cliff Edge? The very same. Hands were shaken. They were delighted to meet him. Cliff for his part was so happy to be the centre of attention again. He kept jiggling up and down and snarling, just as he did in his punk-rock days, exhibiting some at least of the zeal and energy with which, back in the day, he wielded the Stratocaster – his head whipping round again and again whenever something caught his attention. He was really playing up to his desired role. And the twins clearly loved that. They had seen the videos of Suckling Rats bequeathed to them by their parents, and here it was happening in what might be termed real life. We remained seated while conversations between the twins and Cliff proceeded; and meanwhile the rest of the crew assembled themselves: the little pale-faced girl fiddling with the lighting, the youth in dreadlocks with one of the cameras, the other youth with the other camera. Salamanda left the conversation, hung a pair of headphones round her neck and started putting together the microphones and sound equipment. The lighting girl came forward to dab a little make-up on Cliff's face, which he clearly enjoyed. Everything was switched on, the cameras were ready. It had been decided that Cliff would walk up and down on the beach in front of the placid waves as Solomon fired questions at him. So they did, and the crew followed them, step by step, their shoes crunching on the shingle, gradually going out of our earshot. Cliff's shock of hair stood out, a flax-coloured fountain, against the darker sea. We can only surmise that Solomon was questioning Cliff about his notorious past, about his cohorts in the relatively short-lived project that was Suckling Rats – late lamented bass player Shammy Leather, an enigmatic presence, on his own planet; that mad lead vocalist of the staring eyes with whom he, Cliff, all snarls and pouts, had had duelling matches both on and off stage, ah, Petri Disch, that was his name, was it not? that is to say his stage name, drunk on duty much of the time but screamingly brilliant when on form (according to Cliff), who expired years later in the shower at home in a post-binge stupor; and the drummer, whose name no-one could ever remember (it was

Jimmy something) who much later retired to the country to farm pigs and with whom Cliff was still intermittently in touch – but also that Cliff would rather be talking about his current obsessions, including his late love for the music of Scarlatti and Couperin, but principally the theme he returned to again and again, about mobile alien cities traversing the deep, occasionally surfacing on our horizon, cities inhabited by advanced molluscs, octopus-like beings, highly intelligent but with an individual lifetime of only two or three years, tragically passing on their wisdom nevertheless for countless generation on generation over millions of years or maybe even hundreds of millions of years of evolution, unnoticed by us who are supposedly the master race on this planet. We couldn't decipher his words properly at this distance of course, but we could tell from his jerky movements, pointing again and again out towards the horizon where he claimed he personally had witnessed the occasional appearance of such advanced structures as this race of beings had permitted to reach the surface briefly, throwing his arms about in his excitement, warning of this threat to the *whole of fucking humanity* – you know what I'm saying? – if we do not mend our ways; warning that they, the mollusc people, would eventually have to punish us for persistently befouling and eventually destroying the planet on which both races should be living peacefully in harmony. And we might suppose that Solomon asked him: Do you really believe in all this stuff? and that he might have replied, as he did once to us, Not really, mate, but I'm writing a fucking book about it – which was a lie then, and would still be a lie now, because Cliff is incapable of writing a book, which requires hours, days, weeks, months, years of mind-bogglingly tedious study, as he knows very well, and his own temperament is far too up and down, too prone at times to leap into the void, at others to retreat into the gloomiest depths of a mental cave or pit where he does nothing and nobody can see him. But now the crew, led by Solomon and Cliff, were beginning to return from the shore, dodging the intermittent waves as they walked slowly back up the beach, and we could begin to actually hear what they were saying. Solomon was explaining that they had acquired some footage of ancient interviews that could be inserted as flashbacks with Cliff's permission – *[cue rippling harp music]* interjected Salamanda, giggling happily, we'll dub that in, ha ha. And sound and video clips of Suckling Rats, we can put those in, need to secure the rights, obviously. Fuck knows what I was saying back then in them interviews, said Cliff, I was out of me head half the time. Well, said Solomon, we won't do anything without your permission, anyway that was really good just now. But next (turning to us on the bench where we sat patiently) we're going to have a few words with your friend Grech here. At this, Cliff laughed his uproarious laugh. Grech? He told you his name was Grech? Ha ha, that's a good one. I know him as Phil. That's the name he told me he goes by, anyway. And by the way at the Shell Beach Project they call him Colin. Colin! What the hell. He can call himself whatever he likes, far as I'm concerned. Fucking awesome philosopher, whatever his name is. Fucking *deep*. You know what I mean? And how do you know he's a philosopher? inquired Solomon with great seriousness. Because you can't understand a fucking word he says most of the time, asserted Cliff, with a wink in our direction.

Lighting, sound, cameras, all were now focused in this direction. And Solomon began. Now, Grech, just relax, if you think you've made a mistake we can begin again any time you want. Now your friend Cliff says you're a philosopher. So we want to know about your philosophy. When we last spoke, yesterday, you quoted ... ah, who was it? Baudelaire, we offered. Oh yes, that's right, Baudelaire, said Solomon. He went on: Can you say a bit more about your philosophy, Grech? We were nonplussed for a moment. We have no philosophy, we explained, only our thoughts. But thoughts are inalienable – that is to say, not subject to being taken away from or given away by the possessor. They can take away everything from you but your thoughts. Not even the so-called Thought Police can. Unless they have ways to make you really sick. So we are left here on the shore with our thoughts, and it is amusing to let them go where they will and that's all there is to it really. What else can we do?

Would you say something about how you came to be here, living in this place, living the way you are? asked Solomon. To which we replied, Where we dwell now is the beach. It is also known as the universe. The beach, or the universe, chose us, not we it. There it is always, and here it is. The universe does not move. It never moves. It is only the things moving past it or within it that move. But we find it difficult to perceive this. Well, you might say impossible. The universe has many names, perhaps more names than there are atoms within it, who knows. In the manifestation we presently perceive, it is known as the beach, and that is therefore its name for our present purposes. We can't escape from it. Yet the universe may not actually exist. The universe may be a strange loop that simulates itself into existence, so some of the latest scientific thinking suggests. We are getting into some very complicated stuff here. We do not have the resources to pursue this matter much further in any case, because our library has been much depleted. This is our chief regret. We don't mourn our other possessions, but our library was dear to us once. It has been dispersed, and only a few remnants are with us presently. We are only too conscious of this but there is nothing we can do about it. Ah, consciousness ... (we paused here). Consciousness may be embedded in the universe. That is one theory. Einstein believed this. And Max Planck too, look it up, we have not the means presently to check the reference, as I explained. But where were we? Consciousness may be embedded in the universe, that's it. But we have no way of knowing this for sure, since consciousness itself is the way we know things. Consciousness is recursive: for example, it enables us to say things like "Consciousness began when the gods stopped speaking" but this has no more intrinsic meaning than anything else, it takes us no further. Because it is an observation about consciousness made from within consciousness. So it is not a true understanding. Understanding is, if you think of it literally as *standing under*, or standing aside from, not strictly possible with respect to consciousness. You can't stand aside from consciousness and observe it. The ligatures binding us to consciousness are powerful. You could call this a field boundary that stops us seeing too much. A flaw, or a fault, a necessary one, to prevent our breaking down in an endless feedback routine. That way leads only to mental ill health. Which is a fault across consciousness, as Freud said. Again, we cannot verify that quote. We may be misquoting. We need to consult the books. Or the world's oracles. Unfortunately, the public library, along the shore to the east of here, has been shut for some time, due to the spending cuts. There is nothing to be done about that. Apparently. The old double-u double-u double-u dot whatsoever dot com expedient is no longer available, either via that route or any other. But if consciousness is not embedded in the universe, well then, what happens? That is to say, *does* anything happen? The old thing about the tree falling in the forest and no one to hear it. Bishop Berkeley and all that. If there is no perceiver, then it didn't happen. If there is no record, or even if there is a record but there is nobody left to perceive the record, then it didn't happen. Once the last conscious entity has lapsed, then the situation has been reached when history is abolished, when nothing happened. Then none of this happened. Which is absurd. So philosophers have started talking about God keeping it all alive, which is even more absurd. If we are not here on the beach, perceiving it, then it falls to, what, to the gulls to perceive it and thereby ensure the beach is real, or if the gulls decide to migrate, well then the invertebrates crawling around the pebbles, the crustaceans in the shallows, they have the job of keeping the beach real, and if not them, then the single-celled entities, the microbes that are all around us, and if not them, what, the stones themselves? Is the shingle conscious? the shingle, perceiving itself, conscious of itself? Is that how it works? And if the very shingle perceives itself, is its report to be trusted? These are interesting questions, and we have all the time in the world to pursue them here. (But we were quite forgetting by now what the question was that Solomon had posed.)

That's really fascinating, he interrupted at this point, and I'd like to hear more about that, but what I was really after right now was, can you give us any more background to your present circumstances, how a man of your accomplishments came to be living in a tent, on a bench? And we replied, Background? there is no background; everything is foreground. It is very important to understand this. If you don't understand it, you don't understand anything much. Everything is interconnected, there are no entities forming a backdrop for the "real" action (we made what we believe are called "scare quotes" here in the air with the fingers of both hands) or the "significant" (similar gesture) action. People say in passing, when passing the time of day with us here, as some are kind enough to do, though we don't always welcome it, "Oh, it must be so nice to be able to observe nature in peace and tranquillity, the birds and the sea and the fish and so forth," to which we say you misunderstand. We cannot observe nature, because we *are* nature. We are in the middle of it all, all the time. What we call nature is us but also nature observes us as much as ... well, it's all the same thing. Do you see? So no, there's no background, this is all there is, the trail goes back and forth and in and out and up and down, there isn't an end or a beginning, and there's no observation point that everyone can agree on, and what we might tell you one day may not, on reflection the next day, turn out to be accurate or useful after all. All we can know is that we are part of the universe, which is otherwise known to us as the beach. And we are here now, but we were elsewhere previously, and still elsewhere before that, but whether there is cause and effect entailed in that is up for grabs, it might all be chance, but whatever the case there isn't a, what you might say, a hierarchy of significance there. The universe may evolve in time, but some say time is an illusion, so where does that take us?

And we left a space there for Solomon's next intervention, and he obliged: Don't you find it a bit lonely sometimes, Grech, living here on the beach, isn't it a bit too quiet sometimes – don't you find the silence a bit much? No, no, never, we replied immediately, emphatically (we were concerned we were being a little rude here, interrupting him, but he had to be put right), not a bit of it. The first thing that needs to be said is that there is no such thing as silence, and for sure here on the beach there is always something going on, always something to listen to, even in the dead of night, what people call the dead of night, which is not dead of course. Never dead. There are our brothers and sisters the herring gulls, they never quite shut up, and there is of course the rhythmic sound of the waves, those are the obvious ones, but there are sounds within sounds everywhere and at every moment, whether it's shingle shifting on the beach or a flap of paper blowing in the wind or the wind itself on the tent canvas, or a low frequency rumble emanating from a long way away, whatever its origin, and there are of course human voices, you can hear *them* from a long way off, the grunting of the brother fishermen as they work to get their punt ready, sometimes you hear a sneeze in the middle of the night, or a very distant faint moaning which is the sound of someone's car alarm going off somewhere – and sometimes one can discern all the frequencies within every sound if one really pays attention. Sounds within sounds. And at the very centre of sound, it's been sometimes said, one finds soundlessness, which one might want to call silence. But it's not really, because what's not so often said is that at the centre of soundlessness one finds sound again. And so on and so on. We believe this to be so. This is an endless recursion, one of many to be found in the universe. Like fractals. This is our experience anyway. Endless recursions frighten people sometimes because they seem beyond control. If we can imagine a book about our life, call it *Grech*, and on the cover we are pictured sitting here on the beach holding the book, which of course has the cover with the title *Grech* and us shown holding the book, and so on and so on, well, it apparently recedes into infinitude. You know the kind of thing. You could obtain the same effect by erecting twin mirrors on either side of us, facing each other. *Mise en abyme*, it's called, being thrown into the abyss. So far, so far. Well, it doesn't actually go on for ever because for example in the case of the book cover the resolution of the print is finite so the picture eventually gets down to a single dot, a single pixel and after that it vanishes. If you were able to increase the resolution by an extraordinary amount you could go on further, but eventually, eventually you would be approaching the atomic level and way way beyond that the Planck length which is the smallest extent that can possibly exist, and that's the end of it. It's a long way down, as someone once observed. So anyway physics overrides it.

Grech, said Solomon, I can see you have very little in the way of personal possessions, does that bother you? or is it a liberation, which is it? Ah, that is a very good question, we replied. A very good question. We have mentioned the lack of a library, but only because it enabled us once, when it existed, to check or extend our thoughts. But having possessions generally. The thing is that having and being are contradictory impulses. The more you have the less you are. Whether that is an exact binary, whether that can be proved scientifically, is impossible to say. May we suggest the more you are the less you need? Or want? Want has two senses, you know, it means lack and it means desire. They seem like opposites but they are the same thing, that is, they are co-dependent. The moneyed society that prevails, that's our name for it, the moneyed society deploys these twin concepts. It creates lack and it creates desire to remedy that lack, which results in further lack and further desire and further lack, and so on, it's another potentially infinite feedback loop, want resulting in want, want want want, but of course it isn't infinite because it will break down eventually. Eventually it will end in catastrophe. The moneyed society can also be called, with a small linguistic shift, the mono-eyed society. It's the society of what Blake called single vision. The foreground and the background, always. The foreground is the promise and the background is the circumstances that make that promise unfulfillable. Politicians and corporations exploit this. And on it goes. In the days when we had access to information technology we once came across an error message: "The procedure could not be completed because it failed to start." This was both amusing and thought-provoking. The procedure could not be completed, the procedure could not be completed, it repeats, why? because ... why? because it failed to start. The procedure could not be completed because it failed to start. That is very profound. Do you not think?

You may be right, Grech, said Solomon, though it was obvious from his body language that he was a little at sea here, and we don't blame him, we were in danger of going over the unstable cliff edge of sense ourself at this point. Listen, he said, you obviously don't want to talk much about your life, and we respect that, but is there any story you might like to relate, that might throw some light on who you are now? Solomon was obviously fishing here, and it was a choice between accepting the bait in a way that didn't do too much damage or saying nothing at all. So another deep breath was taken. Once, we were in business, we said. We discovered we had a talent for setting up and running businesses. We did not have the talent to create, but we did have the talent to spot creators who could facilitate projects. We were fortunate to have the resources behind us to put all this into practice. We were quite successful. We invested wisely. We made money. We employed people. We gave chances to people, and we were amply rewarded when those creative endeavours blossomed and flourished. But among those who benefited was one whom we shall not name, though he has gone by various names and worked under various guises since. This creation of ours, a monster, a Golem made of clay into which we had breathed life, was consumed with jealousy and resentment from the beginning. He had talent – we'd spotted that pretty early on, we picked him out from obscurity and encouraged it assiduously; he'd been one of the first we'd recruited since making his acquaintance in our student days – and for a long time he handled the creative side of our affairs, but he was tainted by a recurrent crisis of confidence, and began to show inexcusable lapses of attention that put the whole operation and the security and well-being of our other employees at risk. He was married at the time to a beautiful and equally talented woman, an actress and singer, but their marriage started to fall apart under the relentless pressure of his obsessions, not to mention the drinking, for both he and she were escaping into that too; neighbours reported frequent screaming matches and the shattering of crockery, though they were soon reconciled after these episodes, once again presenting a duo of smiling faces to the world. But it got worse. He started referring to her disparagingly to anyone who would listen as Tabula Rasa, a Blank Slate. It's no wonder that she eventually left him. After that his performance became so erratic that, reluctantly, we had to fire him. He didn't take it well. He swore revenge. When we next heard from him he was running a fly-by-night private investigation business from a dingy office in Peckham, and going by the name of Phidias, claiming the spurious legacy of the Golden Mean, which testified to the irrationality of his state of being. Well, then, he started pursuing us. It was an obsession. He pressed charges with the police, he pursued us in the civil courts where we had to devote resources to fighting what a judge at one point termed frivolous if not mischievous appeals. At the same time, allegations began to appear in social media and in anonymous emails – anonymous perhaps, but undoubtedly emanating from him – about our companies and our person, which were totally without foundation but soon took their toll of our reputation and therefore our finances. That shifting character, Phil or Phidias or whatever it is he was now calling himself, was doing everything possible to destroy us. We had to fight back. We won damages. Our lawyers pursued him, and when the money to pay lawyers ran out we pursued him personally, but he had by then absconded from those shabby premises in Peckham, and we heard he had departed for the south coast, hoping to make a new life for himself. He was by then living a hand-to-mouth existence, so we understood. A sad end to what had been a promising career, even a brilliant one. Anything had been possible for him at one time. And we believe still that anything is possible in this mysterious world we inhabit. Anything is possible. And if it's possible it will happen, or it will have happened somewhere, at some time or other. Our colleague Mr Clifford Edgeworth informs us for example that an exoplanet has been discovered where it rains iron. You may like to ask him about that when you interview him again. (But here we had run out of breath, and so we awaited any further questions from Solomon.)

And he obliged. One last one, he said. Yesterday my sister said we wanted to know who the real Grech might be. We're still somewhat puzzled. So could I finish by asking straight out: Who is the real Grech? An impossible question to answer, of course, but can you give us any clues? We sighed. We reflected briefly. Grech is dead, we said at last quietly, without emphasis. Dead? Solomon and Salamanda glanced at each other, you could see amusement in their eyes, but they were startled too. Yes, we added, on an impulse, he died that we might have life. (A resonant statement, that – it just came out, we had not thought about it, but we were pleased with it.) Do tell us more, urged Solomon. The twins were obviously confused, as well as amused and startled. But the light was on us and the camera was rolling again, so we continued. Before our life there was our death, we explained. Our death and, subsequently, our funeral. The funeral of Grech was unremarkable. Do you want to know about it, we enquired, insofar as we can recall? (Solomon urged us on wordlessly.) So we closed our eyes and embarked. We can't say that retrieving the memories, or even reinventing them, was easy, but we did our best. We tried to set the scene. It was a grey day in October. Attending one's own funeral is a rare but not unalloyed pleasure. There can't have been more than a dozen or two of us, we reminisced, arranged in our different dispositions in that deliberately uninspiring, featureless and, dare we say it, *soulless* concrete edifice, purposefully designed to leave everything to the imagination. Photos of the deceased at various stages of his life, unrecognisable to us, flicked up repeatedly on the two plasma screens left and right of the coffin to the accompaniment of low, soothing piped music and, we vaguely recall, the officiating priest's kindly, banal platitudes. He made a lot of the deceased's return to the faith in his last days, a mixture of wishful think-ing and sentimentality – but his attempt to connect the event of that afternoon to the greatest mysteries of eternity fell far short and in fact landed full-square in the realm of banality, we recall thinking as we lay in that coffin. It was a cosy place to be. A little like this tent of ours, enclosed all round, her-metically sealed from the world. A relief from that unspeak-able care home in which we had spent the last years of our life being waited upon and babbling inconsequentially. Wait a minute, interrupted Solomon, you say you were *in* the coffin? Yes, we confirmed, in the coffin and simultaneously an unin-vited guest, an interloper, slipping in through a side door. It was somewhat like that Chinese philosopher who didn't know whether he was a man dreaming he was a butterfly or a butterfly dreaming he was a man. Grech, or a man dreaming he was Grech. Do you follow? (More or less, said Solomon, do go on.) Anyway, it was comfortable enough, even though the coffin was not of the highest quality – from afar it might have had the appearance of mahogany, but we can reveal, from inside knowledge, that it was only veneer over pine or perhaps even MDF. But since we were to be cremated it made no difference, indeed it was wise of those who made the relevant decisions not to waste the money. So there we were, Grech all tucked up in the coffin and not-Grech sitting discreetly at the back of that godawful concrete chapel, observing it all – or alternatively, not-Grech in the coffin and Grech the interloper in the chapel. Who knows? The mourners were already assembled. We knew who they were. We transferred our gaze from one to the other. They were family, mostly. At the front would have been Brunnhilde, the deceased's allegedly delightful dental surgeon (third) wife, strong and silent in her demure widow's garb; with her, accompanied by his French wife, was Simon, his tall, Paris-based son working in finance but soon to take time out to resume his studies and perhaps then head off to another job, whatever it might be; along from them, Alice, his daughter, the only member of the family to speak at the ceremony, who had spent her last ten years in Vancouver finishing her studies, and who, when called to the podium, deftly evaded in her brief eulogy the more insalubrious aspects of her father's life; behind them, the deceased's mysterious brother, who had worked with him in his various enterprises until they collapsed, and had subsequently spent most of his working life in South Africa where he still had a house in a gated community; and then behind them all there was a smattering of acquaintances, not to mention Brunnhilde's dental practice team. We had thought at first we recognised most of the mourners – as mentioned before there were not many more than a couple of dozen of them – but as proceedings continued we became less sure. Their faces became less familiar as that hour elapsed. It was as though their faces became masked. Indeed, at one point it seemed, oddly, as though face masks were being worn throughout the ceremony, and all present therefore were rendered disconcertingly featureless while it lasted.

While all this was going on the only thing we could do was try to search deep in our heart for shared memories of times past. We could not find much. Who was the real Grech? Which was more real? The dead man or ourself? Which was more dead? As solemn music finally accompanied the slow descent of the coffin into the waiting inferno and the curtains began to pull together, we had to conclude that none of that mattered quite so much as had once been thought. The one had ruined the other, but death pays the bills. Both were people who got lost in childhood and do not know the way home. But now the ceremony was over, the mourners were starting to move slowly out of the chapel, most filing past Brunnhilde and her team and offering their personal condolences. We stayed in the background, unwilling to encourage the sharp glances that occasionally flickered in our direction. We could see that some wondered who we were, this non-entity who had not been invited to the funeral but who had attended throughout. Well, we were glad we had come. It had helped. We felt at last we might be free. We didn't know how long that would take. So when the opportunity arose we quietly left the building and embarked on a journey, eventually heading back to the coast. And, to cut a long story short, this is where we find ourself now.

At that point we paused. Brother and sister exchanged a glance. They co-ordinated beautifully, they seemed to function impressively as one. *Cut!* said Solomon.

I don't know what that was all about, in fact there's a lot that's obscure – but you kept our attention, said Salamanda, withdrawing the microphone once more. After a moment of reflection, she added there was "a lot to unpack there". And then after another moment made the further observation, as though she was worried we might have taken this the wrong way, that she *loved* it. Really. Whether she was truly convinced remained unknown. The twins conferred again. You have to give them credit. These young people have all the world before them – they've already conquered half of it, or imagine they have – the power of the imagination is that strong at their age. But while all this uncertainty was in the air, so to speak, that same air was all of a sudden pierced by a raucous guffaw. We hadn't realised Cliff was still around. Sometimes you can't shake the monkey off your back, commented Cliff, but even if you can't, you can always change places, you can always *become* the fucking monkey, d'you know what I mean? It is possible that Solomon and Salamanda did not in fact know what he meant, but his insight was unusually profound here.

Next morning the gulls were absent. The sea was calm, if bleak. Grey was the colour. The air was full of words, but no music. Thought was laggardly. It appeared that we had lost the thread momentarily. Mr Clifford Edgeworth, alternately chewing on a Snickers bar and sipping from one of our bottles of water that he had begged, looked like a ghost at his own feast. He was keeping his own voice supple, he said, just in case it was needed. The world will offer itself to you, we assured him, quoting Kafka as it happens. It was the last day of filming; Solomon was directing operations. He said he wanted us both, Cliff and ourself, to walk side by side slowly along the shore, pretending to be talking, though in the event we were *actually* talking because pretending was impossible. He made us do it again. Salamanda, who had been recording the sound the little waves made as they came in and receded, whispering on the shingle, approached us smiling. She said: Grech, you so remind me of Charlton Heston as Moses in the middle sections of *The Ten Commandments* by Cecil B DeMille. That wonderful beard! Solomon went into hoots of laughter at this; he said: We could make the sea part! How do you mean, asked Cliff. We could make it seem, he explained, as if while you two are walking together the sea parts to let you through, like the Red Sea. How will you do that, asked Cliff. Oh, he said carelessly, CGI will take care of all that, very easy to do these days. Fabulous idea! remarked his sister eagerly, I love it. Let's do it, said Solomon. Yeah, said Cliff. So Cliff and ourself resumed the walking conversation. We pointed out that if the English Channel were made to part it might facilitate the passage of the refugees from France; they could arrive on our shore dry-shod, without having to entrust their lives to fragile inflatable rafts, high seas and the manipulations of criminal entrepreneurs. We had been somewhat obsessed with the fate of the refugees since that incident with the coastguards. We had been hoping day by day the refugees would arrive, looking forward to it like the coming of the barbarians in Cavafy's poem, dimly remembered, imagining that they would have been *a kind of solution.* Yeah, brilliant, said Cliff, yeah, fucking brilliant, in fact I can see them, here they come, them refugees, he said pointing at nothing, I can see all the way to fucking France, man, I can see for miles, know what I mean, we're going to lead them refugees to the promised land, Phil, you and me, fuck me, you know I think I really can see all the way to France, that's it there, amazing, and I ain't *on* nothing now, you know me, I've been straight I've been clean since fucking twenty years ago now, it's what you call a natural high I'm on, you know what I mean, clean living lots of hydration go to the bog regular have breakfast regular home cooking lentils peppers bread proper bread salad the works cut out all that processed shit cut out the chemicals know what I mean that was my last chocolate bar I tell you I don't need that any more fairy footsteps fairy footsteps watch out man here comes a wave that's it you me and the fucking refugees eh Phil magic know what I mean we're recycling our fucking lives you and me on the planet we're living on this fucking beautiful planet with all them shouting birds and animals and it's all so transparent the good clean air all around us know what I mean clean air and clean water and we'll say to them refugees what's ours is yours you're all welcome here let's go yeah I'm turning into a fucking *hippie* in my old age ha ha what do you think of that never thought that was coming mind your step there man and we'll live in harmony you me and the refugees live in harmony with other races you know the octopo- octopo- how do you say it the octopodal beings you know what I mean yeah other intelligences on this planet and other planets out there intelligence *unimaginable* to us completely unimaginable know what I mean where we going now never mind are you OK there? *Cut!* said Solomon.

The crew were starting to pack away their gear. Solomon came up to us. Where's Cliff, d'you know? By now Cliff was absent. He had, we fear, exhausted himself. Well, fantastic, Grech, really good, said Solomon. Yes, *really* good, echoed Salamanda, do let Cliff know we'll be in touch, take care. They both in turn shook us by the hand. We'll be in touch with you too, Grech, they said. And the crew then solemnly lined up to shake our hand in their turn: the little pale-faced girl whose name we learned was Sky, the dreadlocked young man, Marcus, the other fatter young man, Robert, all of whose names were learned too late, but that was the way. It was with mixed feelings that we saw them depart in their OSIRISIS PRODUCTIONS van. They had brought with them a certain excitement. They had shared their lunch with us. They had the enthusiasm of youth, which is of course to be prized as long as it lasts. They evidently saw something in us that is not there. They needed to be indulged. It's quite possible and even reassuring to feel compassion with such young people, to catch a glimpse of the world as they see it, maybe as we saw it once. Yet the filming had become irksome; we prize our peace and tranquility, and therefore we craved an end to this episode. And the end had now come.

9 vectors of morbidity

What happened then? It's what happened before. The crashing sounds, even louder (closer) than before, if anything. What were the gulls doing? Flying up, as before, shouting in outrage – as before. But the crashing did not abate; if anything, it redoubled. The noise woke us, brought us out of the tent, our lingering morning dalliance with Sister Sleep rudely interrupted, afraid for our very life. We could not make sense of it at first, and then reality dawned. The row of beach huts and the garage to our left, previously encircled with temporary metal fencing, were now being demolished in short order in front of our eyes, reduced to firewood and concrete rubble. Clouds of dust hung about. A few shafts of light shot through them. There was shouting, and a good deal of swearing too. The gulls' hysterical reaction didn't help. Birds, as a poet once remarked, make very poor role models. And the gulls are no exception in this regard. They squeaked and yelled, as if to complain *what's going on?* In this, our manor. Yet again. But there was nothing to be done about it. Their protests were futile. The fact was that one by one, inexorably, the beach huts were coming down – new spaces were being opened up.

A boy was painting the new fence black. The noise had long abated. He worked slowly, from right to left. On closer inspection, it was evident that he had his tongue out as he concentrated. A young boy with his hood up. The men (now absent) had erected this wooden fence in the aftermath of the recent demolition. And there it had stood, encircling and shielding the new (un)building site from our gaze, until the boy appeared this morning. The boy did not acknowledge our presence. As we sat on our customary bench, gazing in that direction, watching him paint, we heard a call. We looked around and there was the familiar sight of Will, in his Regatta jacket, with his clipboard and pen under his arm. The call had been: Hi Col, how you doing? He had recently been shortening Colin to Col, and we didn't mind that, but it kept taking us unawares. He sat down on the bench next to us, as was his custom. Hey, good news, he said, you're moving up the list. The list? He smiled at our bemusement. You're moving up the waiting list, don't worry. For rehousing. You remember? There was no hurry, we assured him. That's right, no great hurry, he said, but listen, mate: you can't stay here. You really can't. We admitted as much – we are not stupid, we reminded him. He gestured with his left hand towards the fencing that was even now still being slowly painted black by the boy, from right to left, from right to left. All *that*, you know, he said, the building work that's going to start sooner or later. And we're looking towards the winter now, and you know what that means – we were lucky with the weather last winter, but who knows what the coming one will bring – no, you really can't stay here. Understood, we said. Listen, said Will, come on down to the Project tomorrow, have a hot dinner, you like your hot dinners don't you, and we'll talk over all this a bit further, there are all sorts of possibilities, but we want to know exactly what you would wish. And we want *you* to know that we're thinking of you, that someone is thinking of your welfare. Can't say fairer than that. Well, it was impossible to disagree. From there on, the chat was pleasant, touching on gossip about other users of the Project, touching on politics and football (the latter one of Will's greatest loves), though starting to become a little desultory, finally petering out. And by the time he said his goodbyes and left the boy had almost finished painting the fence.

How can you sit here all day, day after day, Sharonne said, and our answer was: because we think we are at last beginning to get somewhere. She laughed. Do you not get cold sometimes, on the bench or in your tent, aren't you ever cold? When it's cold we shiver, we explained, and when it's warm we sweat. That is all there is to it, that is nature's way of regulating. We feel at peace today. And we took a sip from the thermos flask. God bless you, she said. Then added, when there was no response: You don't like me saying that, do you? No, we replied honestly, we believe in no god or supernatural being. But you believe there is *something*, don't you? she asked anxiously. Something? Yes, something *there*, she said. There is something rather than nothing, we replied, and that is as far as anyone can go. And we added for good measure: So far, so far. Well, said Sharonne brightly, I gotta love you and leave you. The wind's starting to get up again over the next day or two, they say, you take care of yourself. See you tomorrow! It may be a matter of regret that Sharonne's coffee, though nice and hot, is not of the highest quality, but it does come with an admixture of care and concern, and there is that to be said for it, which is a great deal.

High winds returned yet again, as predicted by Sharonne. We spent more time in our tent, reading by the light of the torch. On the occasions we emerged to sniff the air, the results were variable. Grey clouds scudded across the sky. The hours of daylight were slowly contracting again by this time. We felt at peace. A little flock of ringed plovers was observed to move rapidly along the border of the beach, from east to west, darting hither and thither in a delightful way. They are rarely seen in this location. One time we were summoned from our tent by what we fancied were familiar voices heard from afar. At first, we could not fathom where they were coming from, and were starting to conclude that this had been an illusion, an auditory hallucination, or even that we had momentarily fallen asleep in the daytime and these were imaginary voices Sister Dream had presented us with. But then, just as we were about to return to the tent, two figures appeared in the middle distance walking along the coastal path side by side. Angus and Queenie were observed, talking in an animated fashion as they came. In fact, they were having a violent argument. Queenie was crying and shrieking alternately. Angus was shambling and talking in his loud monotone. They approached, but they took no notice of us at all, it was as if we weren't there, passed by as we sat on the bench craning our neck to watch them, still arguing, Queenie still bursting into sobs and jerky movements then shrieking. The argument consumed them entirely. And then they were gone. The peace we'd felt before this eventually returned and was undisturbed for a while. Until we heard another pair of familiar voices. Young male voices, also arguing. It was the brothers, the two youths who had tossed our water bottles around. The shark-faced boys, the baby lemon sharks with dead eyes, prowling around, who had proclaimed that our sort of people weren't supposed to be here. They had been observed in the distance on one or two occasions previously; this time they ventured further into our vicinity. But they did not address us or make eye contact. Like Angus and Queenie, they were totally engrossed in their argument. We resolved to sit it out until they disappeared, which they did eventually, heading off in the direction of the fishermen. We should not have felt so complacent about this. Our anxiety about the youths was not, as shall be related, misplaced. The irony is that, despite all these anxieties, we were feeling freer than ever in ourself. Our thoughts at this time were becoming clearer. A profound burden had been lifted in recent days. We wished we could share this insight with Mr Clifford Edgeworth, ask him for his opinion as to why this might be so, but he was not around, he did not appear – possibly he had entered into one of his deep depressions. Or – another possibility – he had become estranged somewhat from us. Why? He'd been unsettled in the latter stages of the filming, there was no doubt about that. Perhaps he'd become jealous that we had attracted the attention of the film-makers, that the starring role he had imagined for himself had been somewhat tarnished, or had not developed in the way he had fancied it would. He had absented himself when Solomon and Salamanda and their crew were here to say their goodbyes. They had instructed us to convey their good wishes to him, but we had not seen him since, and therefore had not been able to carry out their instructions. So our greater confidence and feelings of peace, despite these anxieties, remained unshared. But then that inevitable something unforeseen (that should have been foreseen) happened.

We should have known, we should not have abandoned the station. The signs had been there. Vectors of morbidity were present. The young sharks had been observed from afar, circling. The sky was empty. The wind blew, just as Sharonne had predicted, the sea was high, crashing and angry, airborne flecks of it even reaching as far as our quarters. We should not have done it, but we did. We should not have, but what was to be done now? Our actions had been driven by our new found resolution about our future direction, by the urge to find the world beyond the sluice again, to assure ourself that it was at least *there*, that it was a manifest possibility, a viable way out of here. We'd been a little too impatient. Could it have waited until another day, another week, or at least until a time of day when there might have been more confidence about leaving our possessions temporarily unattended? But when would that have been? Or might we have had the foresight to cram a few of the more prized possessions into the coat pockets? But we did not. Baggage. How did it come to this? The whole point was to free oneself. So be it. We had abandoned the baggage temporarily and set forth. Did we find it, the sluice? yes we did. If that matters now – which it might. What other occasion would have given us more confidence? we don't know. What other occasion might have been more appropriate? we don't know. Yes, to cut a long story short, we'd found the sluice again. We'd walked along the path next to the beach, the angry waves to our left, walked into the wind, and it took some effort, into the west or south-west where it was blowing from, past the fishermen's station (their boat parked on the shingle), past the place where the railway line starts to curve inland and to abandon the coast, past the rocks that cast no shadow, for the day was of course overcast with fast moving, heavy clouds. Then, as usual, we overshot the entrance – missed it – but realised in time, backtracked, backtracked, and there it was of course – at last, what you might call an aha! moment – the broken (still broken), half hidden gate where you least expected it, behind which was the steep embankment descending to the sluggish water that moved almost imperceptibly in its dark narrow channel in the direction of the sea, towards the tunnel under the beach. What was new here? A supermarket shopping trolley was now half-visible in the water below; it had evidently been propelled down the embankment and abandoned there. The steep embankment was descended with difficulty, leading to the path alongside this channel, the railway bridge ahead of us over the sluice itself; beyond that, on the inland side of the railway, would be the overlooked woodland. So we'd taken the path. We'd proceeded into the darkness, under the bridge, where it stank maybe a little more than we remembered, and out the other side, where the channel disappeared underground; the path into the woodland was more difficult than remembered, tangled with brambles, choked with bracken, in parts congested with accumulated vegetation and rubbish tossed in from on high. But deeper into the little woodland, well, that was a different matter. The calls of the perching birds, as ever, were present. Lichens, among the oldest organisms on earth, were present, coating the rocks and tree trunks. The fragrance of flowering plants was present, filling the lungs. The sounds of human construction and destruction were absent. The crashing of the waves was absent. Fear was absent. So we had spent a brief time there. We'd sat down on a log and consumed a sandwich that had been secreted in our coat pocket. We'd sat and thought. Mainly, we were investigating, gauging possibilities for a longer stay there, scouting a sheltered place to pitch our tent. We were only there a brief time, how long? hard to say, but no longer than was necessary because something made us cut the visit short. Something? The return of anxiety. We do not believe in premonitions. But we knew, we should have known. No matter, there isn't any more to say. We needed to get back to our station. Our thoughts completed, we turned; negotiated our way back under the bridge, climbed the embankment with difficulty, stepped over the broken fence and on reaching the seashore again resumed our walk along the shoreline path. But as we approached the vicinity of our quarters we already knew things were not right. The wind was still high. We thought for an instant those white things flying and fluttering about in the wind were birds. They flew hither and thither in random trajectories, just like creatures without a care. But they were not blood and feather, they were pieces of paper. Pages were blowing past us in the ever strengthening wind, pages we suddenly recognised. We grabbed at one, but it evaded us. Another. We read on it: *Vision, as any sense, depends on its sensory organ – if you lose both eyes, you are blind.* Another missed, another grabbed: *Primary consciousness is immediate, ongoing, present-time consciousness.* There could be no doubt where these pages came from: a book that was, that had been and was no longer, one of the last examples in our library. *If there were to be such a thought it must float entirely free of the system and would be utterly impotent to affect later processing.* We collected these random pages crumpled in our fist for no particular reason, for the cause was lost. Our heart in our mouth, we pressed on, only to behold as we approached our station a site of devastation. The boys, the sharks, had visited. It was surely those two – who else could it have been?

Where our station had been set up, in the immediate environs of the council bench and shelter, there was now a ghastly prospect. It produced in us a weird sensation, as if wires were crammed in our mouth and down our throat. Pages torn out of that familiar book that had once been part of our library were still flying around in the wind, very much like the uncoordinated flocks of birds we'd at first supposed. It would have been impossible to catch many more than those two or three by chance. The blue tent that had been pitched in the lee of the shelter was in a collapsed state, its aluminium framework partly disassembled and the components scattered, the fabric torn in several places, flapping in the wind and bearing an uneven discolouration here and there, brown and black charring, evidence of a clumsy attempt to set light to it. The black rucksack was on its side, half disgorging the remainder of its contents, some of which could not be found at all, and the beige canvas holdall, well, that could not be found at first. It was later spotted on the other side of the chain-link fencing, resting on the railway track ballast, having evidently been thrown over the barbed wire topping the fence (which would have required great force) for no apparent reason. Of course reason had not motivated these actions. Of the blankets, one (the one bearing the motif of a bird) had been flung onto some rocks on the beach, from which it was easily retrieved; the other remained folded on the bench where it had originally been left. The two cushions had also been flung far from the station: one was retrieved from a dip in the shingle on the beach, but the other took more finding and was eventually spotted leaning against the black-painted wooden fence encircling the demolished buildings. It was discovered to be stained, however, and smelt strongly of urine, so had to be set aside for eventual discarding in a council litter bin. The sleeping bag had been unrolled and unzipped, again with great force, leading to the suspicion that the zip may have been broken in the process. There was maybe some trace of urine damage here too, but it was possible that it was salvageable. The towel could not be found. A sodden pair of underpants and two or three lone socks were all that could be found of the spare underwear. Only one T-shirt could be found (trampled underfoot), but then it was remembered the other was presently being worn as an additional layer. The cagoule in its waterproof covering, the gift of Sharonne, could not be found. A pair of eyeglasses, out of their case (which was missing) had been smashed against a rock. The yellow toothbrush was found on the shingle alongside the tube of toothpaste, which seemed to have been trodden on and had disgorged much of its load. The plastic crockery could not be found. An empty pack that had once held tissues was moving around in fits and starts in the wind. Sharonne's thermos flask (the Paisley one today) lay broken on the shingle in a brown pool of cold coffee. The last six-pack of bottled water, bequeathed by Will, was gone, but the individual plastic bottles were later observed scattered far and wide, evidently having been used as grenades, hurled with great force. The plastic torch could not be found. The pair of Minolta binoculars could not at first be found, but then was spotted, located metres away, smashed beyond repair. We had intended to take them with us on our expedition to the sluice, and it was a great pity this had not been done. The dead mobile phone could not be found. The wristwatch could not be found, but that was no loss. The bulky manila envelope was torn open, partly disgorging its contents: what documents or photographs remained was not at first clear, but an effort was made to collect what there was before the wind took it all. At least two notebooks were recovered from the partially capsized rucksack; others could not presently be found. But the wallet was in our pocket, and two of the notebooks as well as sundry pens were also safely in our pocket. As to the remains of the library, the warped cover of the hardback volume of *Towards a Science of Consciousness*, minus its dustwrapper (which was nowhere to be seen) was found under the bench, but most of the contents were missing, hundreds of pages having been torn out, in a procedure that must have been both methodical and savage in equal measure, some of these pages being recognised as those seen fluttering on the wind far and wide. *The Herring Gull's World* paperback had sustained similar damage, though not so severe, only a few of its pages having been torn out; it was found, its cover buckled, on the path several metres away and had evidently been trodden on. The old edition of Spenser's *Shepheards Calender* (Containing Twelve Eclogues Proportionable to the Twelve Months) was nowhere to be found and must be presumed lost. And so it seemed that the last of our library was now finally gone, consigned to the same oblivion as that of Alexandria. This had been a sustained and disciplined operation of destruction, nourished by a motivation that could not even be guessed at. We spent some effort collecting and gathering together what we could of the remainder of our possessions, making as best we could the inventory detailed above. But this exhausted us, and soon we had to sit on the bench for a breather. The bitter and unpredictable wind began, slowly, thankfully, to subside even as we sat. Too tired to walk about any longer, we wrapped ourself (again, as best we could) and sat on the bench, while the distances resolved themselves around us. We consoled ourself that at least our bones remained unbroken. Evening drawing on, and the tent being unusable until its eventual repair or replacement, we would have to make alternative arrangements for passing the night. Our wrapping consisted of the following: keeping the overcoat and woollen hat on, one of the blankets (the one bearing the motif of a bird) was fitted as tightly as feasible around our legs; the other was folded on the bench to form a soft base or support; the no longer zippable sleeping bag was disposed around our shoulders and torso, forming an outer layer (we tried to disregard the faint scent of urine that remained). We arranged ourself in such a fashion that as soon as Sister Sleep began to announce her approach we would be able to swing ourselves, completely swaddled as we were, through one hundred and eighty degrees, that is to say from a vertical to a horizontal position on the bench, laying our head on the one good cushion that remained, and lie there for the remainder of the night in not too much discomfort, provided the wind continued to abate, as it was showing signs of doing. And so pending that eventuality we sat huddled in our temporary shelter and gave ourself up to thought, our favourite pastime. And first we addressed the project. If it can be called that. Whether we were considering giving in to doubt – that was the question we posed ourself. Were we beginning to have some doubts about the validity of the project, which is the name we have given to the life of contemplation we have chosen – no – that has been chosen for us? Travel might have been another option. If we can be said to have had options. A life of travel or a life of contemplation. But the life of the road would have been hard. We might have chosen the road, or had the road chosen for us, we might have rambled along the coast, or even inland, but, to cut a long story short, the sedentary life of contemplation had been selected, not because this was restful but because it offered an opportunity to turn life inside out, like a glove that is pulled from the hand. And also because the options were not plentiful in any case, and because friends and colleagues had gradually fallen by the wayside, in some cases as a result of our fall from grace and favour, in others as a cause of the same, in yet others for random reasons that had nothing to do with all that. And age began to fall heavily on our bony shoulders. So far, so far. And now – we settled ourself on the bench, all swaddled in the fashion described above, to take stock, for we knew the bench henceforth offered nothing – there was no future in it, in other words – but what was to replace it? That was another question. And we daydreamed of the world beyond the sluice, beyond that fat, sluggish, greenish, secret water, beyond the filth and destruction wrought by humans – that mysterious world that humans had some time ago given up penetrating, had neglected and left to the lovely ravages of pure process. (Though by no means any longer a pristine wilderness, there yet remaining all that evidence of accu-mulated human rubbish among the vegetation at its entrance.) We tried to remember the various occasions in the past year when we had succeeded in entering that world, when the portal had become manifest and we were through. We recalled that during the early spring wild garlic (*Allium ursinum*) was plentiful under the knotted trees (chiefly birch and holly) and later, bluebells; and we recalled that the wild garlic is edible (the bluebells not so), and also that there were great clumps of fresh nettles flourishing too in that little haven of scrub and woodland, which are known to be highly palatable as a soup, once plucked and immersed in boiling water to remove their sting, so that, given fire and a suitable pot, nourishment could be derived quite easily from the immediate environment; mushrooms too had been observed at various times, so that, all in all, some form of subsistence was entirely plausible. It was highly doubtful whether the sluice itself was a safe source of food or water, but if its water were boiled, for ablutions as well as for hydration or cooking – well, that would work. That might work. But fishing in the sluice, ah no. No fish could live in that water, and even if they were to be obtained they would likely be monsters filled with toxins, no pearls of any price at all to be found there at all, merely pathogens. But the twin fishermen on the beach a little way from us presently, they could surely be prevailed upon from time to time to supply a small portion of their catch from the sea; admittedly, we had never progressed beyond nodding acquaintance up till now, they being men of few words even between themselves, but they had always seemed well disposed. And we fell to daydreaming, obsessively, of the thickets and where they might be cleared and the places where a tent might be pitched, assuming we were able to get the present one mended, or perhaps even replaced thanks to the good offices of Will and the Shell Beach Project, and where a hollow might be scooped out for the camp fire, ah, *the hollow Echo of my carefull cryes* – how does it go? – and a place where we might sit on a stump and listen to the birdsong and the bird calls, having done so many times on our rare and treasured investigative forays, when the perching birds to be found in that place could be witnessed flickering in the branches, holding their parliaments, bowing and peeping, fluttering and begging, robins, blackbirds, song thrushes, tits, chiffchaffs, wrens, nuthatches and treecreepers, *the carelesse byrds that are privie to the cryes of*, how does it go, ah, it's gone. All gone. Did we hear the nightingale, *Luscinia megarhynchos* if we remember rightly, was it once heard in a thicket when we delayed on one occasion in that place until the evening? but if so only once and never a second time, though then again it may only have been an artefact caused by Sister Dream; perhaps we were mixing it up with a remembered solo many years ago by John Coltrane with Rashied Ali on drums, very similar it must be said. In that place we would of course be beyond the purview of the herring gulls, once loved, our companions on the seashore over the past year or so; all summer they were gossiping and shrieking, they sobbed and yelled; but it has to be said their yells were becoming irksome, they were beginning to get on our nerves, and although admittedly many of them, having done their business and raised another chick or two, were due to make themselves scarce as usual over the coming winter and give us a rest, nevertheless they would not be missed so much or at all were we to have the new companionship of the perching birds. We could learn the songs of the perching birds, and their language, if indeed it is one, that is to say if the language or languages of the perching birds in the place beyond the sluice contains structure – it undoubtedly does – but syntax? yes, possibly, the syntax could be studied. We would be honoured to be accepted into their republic – ah, we are warming to this – it would feel like coming home, we could be breathing butterfly dust rather than particles emitted from machines, we would be a witness there, we would be there to hear the tree fall – *the forest wide is fitter to resound*, that's another one – we could dwell undisturbed in our meditations (to use Will's term, though we don't call it anything) for many years to come, health permitting, yes, for many years, one hopes, undisturbed at long last by ghosts of the past that have irritated our being, leaving all that definitively behind us, that is until Sister Sleep's final visit (hopefully unaccompanied by Sister Dream) would put paid to it all. Would there be regrets? Would the ministrations of Sharonne, for example, be missed? After all, Sharonne could not be expected to penetrate the world beyond the sluice, a far cry, that, from the short walk from her house every morning bearing a replacement thermos flask; but to tell the truth, we could easily brew our own coffee in a pot with boiled water from the sluice; but to tell the truth again, the endless charity was beginning to become irksome, one suspects for the giver equally as for the receiver, though neither would find it easy to admit it publicly, and the move contemplated could well be the occasion to say goodbye to all that with at least some grace, each party taking leave with goodwill and good memories remaining; but to tell the truth yet again, this section of the beach was already finished for us; already, people were running around shouting all over the place, and it would only get worse; already, the signs of "redevelopment" were becoming clearer and clearer, the building work would no doubt soon be starting in earnest, this bench and shelter would soon be designated out of bounds prior to being entirely demolished, and we would have been eased out of our station in any case. And as we were musing thus in the gathering gloom, on the horizon of the now much calmer sea some lights slowly became visible, lights emanating from a dark shape on the edge that could not easily be made out in detail, and we reached for the binoculars – but we had forgotten! the binoculars were gone now, damaged beyond repair, so the detail remained forever unobservable, the lights remained blurs, though the structure was definitely still there, and we fell to thinking about our friend Mr Clifford Edgeworth and his unstable theories of cephalopodic intelligences inhabiting marine cities, and a rueful smile may have touched our lips when considering whether he could ever be induced to visit an encampment deep in the wood – he probably would not. So far, so far. And all this was written down in one of the remaining notebooks while dusk was coming on and while there was still light enough to see.

A shelter stands at the top of the shingle beach, once provided by the Council for the convenience of members of the public using the path that tracks the beach on the one side and the railway on the other. Its stanchions, and the bench that forms an integral part of the structure, are, we know, painted green – to be more precise, Buckingham Green – but the light is presently too poor to discern the exact colour. There is nobody about. At present, no individual is availing themself of the shelter; no one is sitting on the bench. The fact, however, is that no one would be able to do so without difficulty, because it has been wrapped around by the authorities with criss-cross warning tape, designating it as out of bounds, pending demolition. Now this is the hour before the first light of day. The twin fishermen to the west have already begun their day's activities, making their way silently to and from the island of low broken buildings out of which they work, prior to launching their little boat from the beach. They don't say much: just a low grunt maybe, now and again. Very occasionally what may be construed as a groan. By this time some of the herring gulls that nest hereabouts on the sundry remaining buildings that fringe the shoreline have begun to give voice too, perhaps articulating frustrations of various kinds. The sky above is indigo, the east reddish. All of this is of course part memory part imaginative speculation. Presently, a creaking sound heralds the approach of a cyclist on the shoreline path, the light in the gloom bobbing now with the unevenness of the surface, the periodic breath becoming more audible with the approach; and he sweeps past the empty shelter and vanishes, creaking still, in the direction of and then past the mountains of rubble standing in place of the garage and beach huts that formerly fringed the shore along here. These piles are protected by wooden fencing that has been erected all around them, painted black, with appropriate warning notices affixed, but also already bearing the mysterious ideographs of rudimentary graffiti. And in between the graffiti another new notice: *COMING SOON: Twenty-four luxury holiday and family homes, comprising one- and two-bedroom flats and three-bedroom houses*, it says. After a short while, the first train of the day, to be heard rumbling in the distance, quickly approaches from the east, rushing past and then vanishing with a Dopplered roar into the west (which is the up direction), and this instantly fixes the time at 06:13. There will then be an estimated five to ten minutes to wait for the sunrise.

So far, so far.

epilogue

new independent film features a cameo role for Unstable Cliff Edge, former lead guitarist and song-writer with the legendary Seventies punk band Suckling Rats, who plays himself and whose music also forms part of the soundtrack from time to time. The movie, *Grech*, is on release now. The main character, however, is Unstable Cliff Edge's friend, an elderly beach dweller known only as Grech, whose philosophy is expounded at length during the course of the film. We follow the eponymous Grech and Cliff in their quest for a benevolent alien civilisation across the sea – in one scene they are pictured marching towards the horizon, fording the waters of the English Channel like Moses and Aaron crossing the Red Sea in Cecil B DeMille's *The Ten Commandments*, aiming to lead a band of boat refugees to the promised land. This may be the least convincing sequence in an otherwise remarkable film. The twin brother-and-sister directing team, Solomon and Salamanda Evans, worked with real people in this seaside town, rather than profes-sional actors, and the film makes use of improvisation, with little or no scripted dialogue. Salamanda Evans' haunting ambient music, mingling with the cries of gulls, is often the only sound. The present circumstances of the character known as Grech are not known for certain, and he did not turn up for the premiere. It was reported that he had become nervous about being plagued by visitors following his leading role in the film, and that, in the wake of the pan-demic of 2020-21, he had been resettled in his own flat with the help of a local charity, the Shell Beach Project (who have refused comment). But other reports suggest he instead retreated to and established a camp in dense woodland beyond a sluice that empties waste water into the sea a little way west of the beach where he had previously lived.

Grech is available on various digital platforms.

Also available from grand**IOTA**

Brian Marley: APROPOS JIMMY INKLING
Ken Edwards: WILD METRICS
Fanny Howe: BRONTE WILDE
Ken Edwards: THE GREY AREA
Alan Singer: PLAY, A NOVEL
Brian Marley: THE SHENANIGANS
Barbara Guest: SEEKING AIR
Toby Olson: JOURNEYS ON A DIME
Philip Terry: BONE
James Russell: GREATER LONDON: A NOVEL
Askold Melnyczuk: THE MAN WHO WOULD NOT BOW
Andrew Key: ROSS HALL
Edmond Caldwell: HUMAN WISHES/ENEMY COMBATANT
Ken Edwards: SECRET ORBIT
Giles Goodland: OF DISCOURSE
Rosa Woolf Ainley: THE ALPHABET TAX
John Olson: YOU KNOW THERE'S SOMETHING
James Russell: THE GRIFFIN BRAIN
Brian Marley: ON REFLECTION
Eric Mottram: BLOOD ON THE NASH AMBASSADOR
Sharon Kivland: ALMANACH

Production of this book has been made possible with the help of the following individuals and organisations who subscribed in advance:

Rosa Ainley
Aris Anagnostopoulos
Tony Baker
Christopher Beckett
Paul Bream
Andrew Brewerton
Ian Brinton
Jasper Brinton
Hamish Buchanan
Thomas Carroll
Rosie Dastgir
Sam Dolbear
Susan Finlay
Allen Fisher/Spanner
Benjamin Friedlander
Paul Green
Penelope Grossi
Leopold Haas
Michael Hampton
Randolph Healy
Lindsay Hill
Jeremy Hilton
Gad Hollander
Fanny Howe
Elizabeth James
Lauren Kalita
Alexandra Keramidas
Ian Land
Sophie Lee
Katharina Ludwig

Julia Luebbecke
Murdo Macdonald
Michael Mann
Michael Maranda
Eleanor Margolies
Timothy Mathews
Rod Mengham
Paul Nightingale
Joseph Noonan-Ganley
John Olson
Irene Payne
Sean Pemberton
Bridget Penney & Paul Holman
Frances Pinnock
Samuel Regan-Edwards
Adrian Rifkin
Elaine Rose
Lou Rowan
Assunta Ruocco
James Russell
Valerie Soar
Zoe Skoulding
Gavin Traeger
Keith Tuma
Roxy Walsh
Keith Washington
Tony White
Isobel Wohl
Shamoon Zamir

www.grandiota.co.uk